MW01165615

Debra L. Krill
2011

Winds Across the Prairie

By

Debra L. Hall

Author of the Easterner.

authorHOUSE

1663 LIBERTY DRIVE, SUITE 200
BLOOMINGTON, INDIANA 47403
(800) 839-8640
www.authorhouse.com

First published by AuthorHouse 04/06/04

ISBN: 1-4140-5262-6 (e)
ISBN: 1-4184-2265-7 (sc)

Printed in the United States of America
Bloomington, Indiana

This book is printed on acid-free paper.

Cover concept and design by Debra L. Hall

Graphic Artist and photographer of the author: Alyce M. Williams

Dedication

This story is dedicated with love to

Dorothy Hall and Ruby Richards

With special thanks to

Ivy and Iris Halverson

And to those who proof read and or offered editorial advice:

Amy Davis, Eleanor Hall, Rebecca Addy, Leona Tippit, to Theresa Hammond Parker for an excellent job of critiquing, and to Travis D. Hall for prose introducing chapter one.

The winds blew them across the prarie
Their hearts,
Their dreams,
Their very souls

TABLE OF CONTENTS

CHAPTER ONE

Nebraska
Spring 1868

Lively eyes of youthful fire
Swept aside by fated ire

"Iris! Wait! Come back!" Edward Stratton stood up in the stirrups and shouted across the swelling prairie. "Blast it all! If she's not a stubborn Rutledge I don't know what she is." He fell back into his saddle, frowning. What possessed him to say that? He hadn't thought of Iris' mother for weeks. He looked up just in time to see his daughter gallop over the last swell against the horizon. There was no use going after her. What he said upset her, and for good reason. He gathered the reins in, turning his horse around before nudging her flanks.

A short time later he walked out of the barn toward the house. There was no sign of Iris' horse, which meant she probably wouldn't be back until after sundown. He didn't know why she...

"Where's Iris?"

The screen door padded shut and Edward's sister, Emma, stepped onto the wide porch with her hands in the pockets of her gardening apron. Edward took off his hat and pushed his spread fingers through his graying hair. He grimaced, rubbing his taut neck muscles.

"She worked herself all up into a frenzy, then rode off toward the creek."

"So, you told her then." Emma swept her hands across the front of her apron. "I'll go talk to her," she said. Opening the door she grabbed her shawl off the wooden peg. The door creaked shut as she descended the wide steps.

"You can save all that woman talk for later. I'm hungry."

"You're always hungry, so go inside and eat." Emma walked past him, adjusting her shawl as she headed toward the

1

foot path that led to the creek. "Your plate's on the table." She called over her shoulder. "Stella can wait on you."

Edward groaned. "That girl's at least as stubborn as her Aunt."

Iris Stratton lay back in the fresh spring grass with her arm draped across her forehead to keep the sunlight out of her eyes. "I won't do it," she complained to herself. A moment of quiet passed and Iris thought how good the warm sun felt. She squinted above the crook of her arm at the milky white clouds being dragged across the blue sky by a soft fragrant breeze. She sighed, mesmerized by the smell of wildflowers and the thought of the earth yawning after a long winter's rest. Rolling over she opened her book of Tennyson poems and whispered the words softly to herself.

"Clearly the blue river chimes in its flowing
Under my eye;
Warmly and broadly the south winds are blowing
Over the sky.
One after another the white clouds are fleeting;
Every heart this May morning in joyance is beating
Full merrily;
Yet all things must die."

She slammed the book shut and sat up, throwing her hands out. "But I'm too young to die!" Her eyes quickly scanned the blowing grass half expecting to see the intruder creeping toward her this very minute. "He's so loathsome. What am I going to do?" She pressed her clasped hands into her chest where they supported her chin. Biting her lower lip she sniffed back the urge to cry. "I'll run away," she concluded. "It's the only... Ohhh!" Her fingers flew to her trembling lips. She couldn't leave her father. But she would rather die than marry Leo Branson. Her breath escaped as she dropped her shoulders. Surely her father wouldn't make her marry a man she didn't love.

Iris' horse, Honey, came up next to her and nibbled the sweet grass. She neighed softly then brushed her velvety muzzle down Iris' arm and into her hand. Iris petted the horse's quivering nose. As she reached for the dangling reins, she saw someone in the distance walking along the foot path. Although the figure was a long way off, Iris could tell that it was her Aunt Emma by the way the sun reflected off her chestnut colored hair knotted loosely at the nape of her neck.

"If she's going to try to convince me to marry that disgusting excuse for a man then she's wasting her time," Iris scowled. Deciding to ignore the subject altogether, she continued reading her poetry.

At a moment when Iris felt the most confident in her convictions, knowing that a secret was hidden safely in her heart, the book fell open exposing the words that she read everyday, the words that were once breathed passionately into her ear by the only man she could ever truly love. Her fingers lightly touched a cluster of pressed violets that Andrew had given to her over a year ago. He said they were the color of her eyes, just before he kissed her cheek then left to go back to Boston. Her throat constricted and her eyes blurred until a large tear plopped onto the page. Wiping her eyes with the back of her hand she read aloud, her voice quivering.

"Now folds the lily all her sweetness up,
And slips into the bosom of the lake.
So fold thyself, my dearest, thou, and slip
Into my bosom and be lost in me."

"Iris. Iris, what's the matter? Why are you crying?"

Iris looked up at the bleary figure of her aunt moving toward her. She wiped her eyes on her sleeve, sniffing loudly. "I'm not...crying...I...Ohh! Aunt Emma I can't help it. I get so angry when father starts talking about me getting married."

Emma sighed deeply just before she sat down in the grass beside Iris. "I know, dear." Reaching out she smoothed back a strand of Iris' black hair. "Look at your face all smudged with tears. Your father will think himself an ogre if he sees how upset you are."

"I don't see why he has to bring all this up when the picnic is Saturday. Now, I won't have an ounce of fun."

"Of course you will," Emma consoled.

Iris shook her head, drawing her hand under her nose. "I'll never have fun, not ever again in my whole life."

Emma pulled a handkerchief from her sleeve and handed it to Iris who promptly blew her nose. "Your father didn't say that you had to marry Leo Branson. All he said was, that Leo spoke to him. The Bransons are coming over tonight since it's the proper way to discuss proposals, whether they're accepted or denied."

Iris quickly drew back. "I won't be there! I'll run away if I have to. I..."

Emma swiftly took Iris' hands in hers. "Iris, please, try to understand that this meeting has to take place. You know that your father won't make a decision without consulting you first. He's always cared about how you feel. Sometimes too much, if you ask me."

Iris pulled back her hands, lacing them tightly against the side of her face. "Then he should know how much I despise Leo Branson, and how horribly rude I think he is."

"Men don't always consider such things. Iris, you're already sixteen, and your father's not a young man anymore. He's growing concerned about your future."

Iris burst into tears that she quickly fought to control. "I won't have a future if father makes me marry a man that I don't love. Especially a man as ugly as Leo."

"Oh, Iris, really."

"It's true." She cried disparagingly. "His shoulders are thick and stooped, and his nose looks like a bee stung it, and his...his hair's the color of dirty water. Haven't you ever seen how disgusting it looks when he puts that grease on it to keep it down? And to make it even worse he ties it back with a piece of rope."

"Looks aren't everything."

"You wouldn't say that if he was going to talk to your father about you." Iris angrily batted away her tears. "He has a long blue scar on his neck that's so grotesque my skin crawls whenever I look at it. Rebecca told me a trapper once tried to stab him when he was caught stealing furs."

Emma shook her head in disapproval. "You shouldn't listen to such stories."

"But it's true," Iris shuddered. "I cringe every time he looks at me with those deep, dark eyes that blatantly reveal his lewd thoughts."

Emma's back stiffened, her hands clasped tightly under her breasts. "His lewd thoughts...such talk." Her lips pursed for a silent moment before she mildly scolded. "You have a wild imagination, that's all."

Iris swiftly came to her feet, the book of poetry clamped tightly against her chest as she walked toward her horse. She picked up the reins then turned around to look at her aunt who was just standing up. "That's not true. I mean, I do have a colorful imagination, like you said, but everything I've said about Leo Branson is true. You've just never seen the way he looks at girls."

Emma huffed while smoothing down her skirt. "Well, if it's half as bad as you describe it then I hope to God that I never do. Nevertheless you be civil to the Bransons tonight, do you hear me?" Without waiting for a reply Emma started down the path. "I want you to come home right away."

Iris drew Honey along by the reins while she followed after her aunt. "But Rebecca's suppose to come over tonight. We were going to hem her dress for the dance."

Rebecca Archer had been Iris' friend since childhood. They did everything together, and Iris wasn't about to let Leo Branson come between them.

"Since when did you start caring so much about wearing dresses?"

"It's not that I don't like wearing dresses. I just don't like wearing them all the time."

"There will be plenty of time for hemming dresses after

5

the Bransons leave. Right now you need to get out of those unsightly britches and put on your blue poplin."

"Good. That one has a high collar."

"And comb that unruly hair of yours. You look like a wild Indian."

"I wish I was an Indian. Then I could..."

"I'll have none of that kind of talk! You just do your hair up nice, the way I showed you so you'll appear presentable."

Iris' eyes filled with despair. "But I don't want to appear presentable."

"It means a lot to your father to be well spoken of Iris."

When Aunt Emma said things like that Iris found herself at a loss of words. She'd been told often enough how hard it was for her father to raise her without a mother, even though to Iris her aunt was as good a mother as any. They walked the rest of the way home in silence while Iris plotted inconspicuous, lady-like ways to convey her feelings of loathing to Leo Branson.

CHAPTER TWO

A twilight breeze slipped through the parted curtains and into the well-arranged parlor that appeared dwarfed once the men entered the room. Iris was sitting prim and proper on a straight back chair across from the window with her hands folded in her lap and her eyes downcast enough for her to appear submissive. Her insides belied the calm she had practiced to perfection. Her stomach rolled then fell where it settled into a knotted lump between her ribs, while her chest barely moved as every breath was being forced from her lungs. Despite the cool breeze coming through the windows she could feel the warmth of her taut body rising to her face. She desperately hoped, since she had put her hair up, as instructed, that it hadn't become obvious to anyone in the room that her ears were turning red. In no way did she want Leo Branson to assume that she was blushing because he was sitting opposite her. She refused to look in his direction. Still, she could feel his eyes slowly rake over her. He was no doubt inspecting what he presumed would soon belong to him. What he didn't know was that, in a few minutes, when her father and Mr. Branson turned their attention to the subject of marriage and it was her turn to speak, his vivid imaginings would be whisked right out of his decrepit mind.

For the moment her father and Mr. Branson were conversing, their weighty voices droning back and forth across the room in a monotone fashion that told Iris nothing of consequence was being said. Feigning interest, Iris cast her dutiful gaze upon Leonard Branson. He was somewhat older than her father, the years showing in his shaggy brows hovering above faded eyes that lacked expression. Her father's face was smooth and firm, where Leonard's displayed deep lines resulting in flabby jowls. She couldn't help but think how much he looked like a bull. His cheeks were too broad for his bald head that prominently displayed a band of white from his hat line. His ears were big and droopy, like a mule's. She imagined one of them flicking when the fly that was buzzing around the room came near his face. She had to force the thought from her mind or burst out in unlady-like laughter. Since she was making a thorough appraisal she decided that if the hair circling over his ears and around the back of his head was trimmed neatly like her father's he wouldn't appear quite as unkempt. And if he sat up straight instead of sitting slump shouldered in his chair he would look much taller, and not as round as he appeared. Only just then did she realize which side of the family Leo got his nose from. She was surprised that both Mr. Branson and his son had seen the need to dress in their suits, which despite the fact that they were wrinkled weren't the worn over-alls they usually wore. At least Mr. Branson thought it necessary to shave before paying such a visit.

The analysis grew quite wearisome, forcing Iris to look away. All too quickly she grew hypnotized by the sound of the clock ticking on the mantel, then by the swirled pattern of rose cabbage flowers on the carpet. When the curtains billowed she couldn't help but glance through the window at the swaying cottonwood trees that bordered the plowed fields a short distance from the house. All at once she heard the front door thud shut followed by the faint sound of Rebecca's voice then Stella's muffled reply. Iris pictured Rebecca springing freely up the stairs while she was forced to sit as lifeless as a fence post and listen to grown ups plot her dull future.

How much longer would it be before she could take a deep breath?

"And what are your thoughts on the matter, Miss Stratton?"

Iris heard Mr. Branson's question but she had no idea what he and her father had been talking about. She coyly replied, "It's all so sudden I'm afraid I find myself at a loss of words."

"That's why the Bransons are here, dear. To talk over the matter."

Iris looked at her aunt who sat as tall and refined as she. The guarded look her aunt flashed in her direction demanded her rapt, undivided attention. Iris' chin went up and she held her shoulders as square and still as the hanger from which the dress she was wearing had come. After a moment or two passed, where Mr. Branson reminded her father that they've known each other for over twenty years, the conversation swayed to other farmers in the community and how long they had known them. There was a slight tap on the door just before it opened and Katie, one of the tenant farmers daughters, who helped in the kitchen, appeared.

"Excuse me, Miss Stratton. Stella would like to know if you're ready for coffee."

Emma nodded while Mr. Branson said something about the price of cattle after which his son stated a figure. Growing bored with the subject Iris' eyes strayed back to the window where she could see the horses frolicking in the corral to the side of the barn. Listening to the soft cooing of a mourning dove she felt a moment of calm that was soon interrupted by the gruff voices of men outside who were coming in for the night. Iris' shoulders drooped with envy. How she wished that it was her out there running in the wind with the horses instead of sitting as still and straight as a broom in a stuffy closet. With the spring planting nearly completed her thoughts turned to the dance. All of their friends would be there laughing and telling stories or making plans for the summer. Her father had put some of the men to work building a dance platform near the barn and by tomorrow they would have it finished. Dancing was nearly as fun as riding Honey in the wind. It didn't matter then if she held herself straight like a lady. Her attention was drawn back into the room when she heard Mr. Branson clear his throat, shuffle uneasily in his chair, and remark:

"When the Stevens boy brings those horses in things are going to change around here; you can bet on it. It's good to plan ahead, as you well know."

Iris looked at her father, wondering if the time had come at last. His face seemed a bit drawn but other than that he appeared in control, as usual.

Leo's stilted voice filled the room. "John's friend from back east is over at the Stevens' place now building a corral."

Iris' eyes lighted up. Could he be talking about Andrew Burgess?

"We're talking a lot of horses here," Leonard commented with a nod of certainty.

The door opened carefully and Katie entered, carrying a tray. She moved quietly from one person to the next offering potica cake and coffee, which Iris declined. When Katie came to Edward he put his hand up when his cup was half full. "You want to be a part of what's coming then?" he asked in a controlled voice.

"I want us to be a part of what's bound to happen to the midwest," Leonard Branson replied.

Edward took a sip of his coffee, remaining quiet with his head bent down. After a long deliberating moment he looked up. "And what's that?"

"Growth, as far west as we can go," Leonard replied stoutly.

The room was just beginning to grow dim when Emma rose uneasily and began lighting the lamps while motioning for Katie to draw the curtains. In the last bit of daylight, just before the windows thudded shut and the heavy curtains devoured the lace sheers behind them Iris saw, beneath her raised lashes, Leo Branson's eyes following the contour of Katie's lithe form. Iris' mouth gaped open and for a moment her breath caught in her throat. What an insufferable lout! If only her aunt would turn around. This would probably be her only chance to see how disgusting Leo Branson really was. But her aunt never turned her head. Iris watched Katie flit out of the room carrying the tray, her thoughts of utter disbelief blasted from her mind when suddenly she heard Mr. Branson's baritone voice bellow.

"We made an agreement, Stratton, or have you forgotten the promise you made sixteen years ago?"

Iris had never heard Mr. Branson speak to her father like that before. What promise was he talking about? Quickly she looked at her aunt for reassurance but Emma's eyes were fixed firmly on her brother, her hands wringing in her lap as she fidgeted closer to the edge of her chair. A flash of wild disbelief ripped through Iris, leaving her feeling weak and flushed. He couldn't be talking about Leo Branson's proposal. That only happened a few days ago. Had her father and Mr. Branson talked of their children marrying sixteen years ago...when Iris was born? Surely not! Her eyes flashed across the room where they were met by Leo Branson's rapacious smile. No! She began to shake visibly while her heart was near to bursting. Her throat knotted to hold back the tears that threatened to gush. She couldn't leave home, not now. She wanted to be with her father when he painted wildflowers in the fields. She wanted to look over his shoulder when he finished sketching the windmill that was here long before he came to Nebraska, years before she was born. She didn't want to be anywhere near Leo Branson, much less trapped in his arms while his covetous eyes hovered above her. Her stomach lurched, making her feel nauseous.

Edward's cup and saucer clattered onto the side table and Iris gasped audibly when he flew forward in his chair, his full attention on Leonard Branson.

"All we ever talked about was our land. I never made you a promise, and you know it Branson. You took advantage of a man who was out of his mind."

"You're not out of your mind now, are you?" Leonard Branson's challenging insult seemed to reverberate off the papered walls flying straight toward Iris who swayed slightly to the right.

Emma sprang to her feet, her sharp words directed at her niece. "Iris! Go to your room!" Iris sat dumbfounded staring at her aunt and then at her father whose face was white with anger. "Now!" Emma commanded. She flew across the room and grabbed Iris by the arm, hustling her out of the parlor and into the hallway, where she clicked the door shut tightly behind her.

Iris gasped when the last thing she heard was Mr. Branson shouting at her father.

"You said, if our children married we could join properties and push west as far as land and money would allow."

Iris' chest was heaving and she fell heavily into the wall next to the door. Shocked, she vaguely heard her father's reply.

"It was a whimsical comment, not a contract. You knew it then and you know it now. You have no right to come here and insinuate..."

Hearing the parlor door open, Katie appeared from the kitchen. "Rebecca is here, Iris. She's waiting upstairs." Katie stopped abruptly when she saw Emma fanning Iris' flushed face with a handkerchief. "Should I get some water?" she asked, concerned with the sudden turn of events.

Emma muttered a reply and Iris' eyes went from Katie who was headed back into the kitchen to those of her aunt's that were clouded over with indignation.

"Why did father say that he was out of his mind?" Iris pleaded.

Quickly Emma looked at the parlor door then back at Iris. "It's late, Iris. You need to go to bed."

"Tell me, Aunt Emma, please. What happened sixteen years ago? Did father tell Mr. Branson then that Leo could marry me when I grew up?"

Angry voices filtered through the door.

"If you sign an agreement he'll wait until she's eighteen."

"No! You took advantage of my unfortunate situation."

Emma's face was stern. "No," she stated flatly. She took Iris by the crook of her arm and began ushering her up the steps.

"Please tell me what's happening. I'm not a child," Iris stubbornly insisted.

"It doesn't concern you now, Iris. It was a long time ago."

Iris looked back over her shoulder.

The kitchen door thudded shut and the sound of Katie's shoes snapping rapidly on the flagstone floor echoed through the entryway. There was a moment of silence as Katie hustled nervously up the carpeted stairs carrying a glass of water which Emma turned and quickly intercepted before dismissing her. Emma waited on the landing until Katie was downstairs before she directed her full attention to Iris. Carefully she placed the glass in Iris' trembling hand, waiting until Iris had a firm grip before she let go.

Iris took a sip then quickly said, "But it does concern me. They're down there talking about my future."

Peering intently at Iris' face Emma chose her words carefully. "There's no need to worry. Your father would never do anything to jeopardize your happiness." Emma looked down the stairs where the sound of irate voices hovered near the landing. "Go change out of your dress and then help Rebecca with her hem before it's too late."

"But..."

"Go on now," Emma's voice was firm.

Iris walked a short distance down the hall then turned the door knob and slipped into the muted light of her room, wondering if in fact it was too late.

CHAPTER THREE

Iris was not in the mood to hem dresses and, in fact, didn't care if she ever wore a dress again in her life. She stood with her ear pressed tightly against the door while Rebecca, unaware of what had taken place downstairs, kept chattering about ruffles and how bits of lace sewn in just the right places drove men mad. Iris frantically motioned for her to be quiet, thinking Rebecca could drive a man mad without adding lace to her dress. Not able to hear clearly what was being said downstairs she turned around sharply, ready to scream when she was met by Rebecca's dour expression closed in by her long honey colored hair that was sticking out in all directions.

"What happened to your hair? You look like a wild woman."

"Nothing. I didn't have anything else to do so I was brushing it out."

Disgruntled, Iris mentally scolded herself for being so abrupt. "I'm sorry, Rebecca. But everything's going wrong." Just a few hours ago she had been excited about going to the dance and now she didn't care if she ever left her room again. Resignedly she sighed. "Wait until I get my dress off and I'll braid it for you." Iris' fingers tore at the buttons trailing down the front of her bodice.

"They're down there planning my destiny. Mr. Branson is trying to trick my father into an arranged marriage."

"You mean you and Leo Branson?" Rebecca's face drained of all color.

"Yes! They're talking about it now! And..." Iris jerked her skirt over her head. "I need to know what they're saying."

Rebecca's brows came together. "What were they hollering about?"

Iris fumbled with the ribbons down the front of her batiste camisole. "That's what I can't figure out. First they were talking about nothing in particular, and then Mr. Branson said something about some horses, and before I knew it he was threatening my father over something that happened sixteen years ago."

"That's when you were born!"

"I know! That's why it's all so confusing. Mr. Branson said something about a promise, and then..." Iris whirled around. "Rebecca, my father said that Mr. Branson took advantage of him when he was out of his mind."

"Out of his mind. What does that mean?"

"I don't know," Iris sharply replied. "I asked Aunt Emma and she wouldn't tell me."

Rebecca's brown eyes sparkled with curiosity. "What did they say after that?"

Iris shrugged. "Aunt Emma hurried me up the stairs so fast I felt like I'd been caught in a cyclone."

Iris quickly hustled out of her corset then slipped her nightgown over her head. She climbed into her flowered wrap and reached for Rebecca's brush. Moving across the room toward her dressing table she said, "sit over here and let me fix your hair."

Rebecca didn't move, her eyes remained fixed in thought. "Wait! I have a better idea."

"But your hair ..."

"That can wait." Rebecca's hands clasped in front of her. "I have an idea. Maybe Mr. Branson saved your father's life a long time ago and now he wants your father to agree to the marriage as payment."

"Maybe father did have some type of an accident. Otherwise why would he say he was out of his mind?" Iris' face held a confused expression.

"Let's sneak outside and listen at the parlor window. That's the only way you're going to find out the truth." Rebecca urged.

Enlightened by the prospect Iris said, "But I just took my dress off."

Convincingly Rebecca replied, "That's okay, no one will see you."

Iris' eyes flew to the door as though they'd already been

caught. "But how? Aunt Emma just went into her bedroom."

Rebecca scurried to the door and slowly pried it open. Iris thought she must have had a lot of practice in sneaking around because the hinges didn't even squeak, the way they usually did. A draft from the hall swept into the room causing the flame in the lamp to flicker, casting ghostly shadows across the floor and up the walls where they weaved their way through the floral pattern on the paper. Wide-eyed, her imagination ran rampant. Iris' eyes grew larger by the moment. She looked from the yawning shadows on the wall over to Rebecca. A lingering draft from the hall bloused beneath Rebecca's gown then slipped through her hair, stirring it gently, creating wavering, snake-like shadows on the wall behind her. Iris whispered loudly for her to come back, her voice squeaking nervously. Rebecca flapped her hand behind her back for Iris to be quiet.

All at once Rebecca disappeared around the corner.

Iris shuddered, gripping the front of her gown. "Rebecca, wait!"

Rebecca was already creeping down the dark hall.

Iris stood as still as a statue.

A minute of silence passed while the shadowy room absorbed the sound of Iris' pounding heart. The clock on the mantel downstairs struck nine times while Iris felt herself breaking out in a cold sweat. Where was Rebecca? What was she doing? Then suddenly she appeared in the doorway, motioning for Iris to follow her. Iris fluttered to the door where she put her shaking hand on Rebecca's shoulder.

"Where have..."

"Shh!" Rebecca swiftly covered Iris' mouth with her hand. Bending closer she spoke in a hushed tone. "Your aunt's asleep."

Leaning around the door frame Iris peered down the hall where she saw a line of light under her aunt's bedroom door. She pulled back Rebecca's hand and speaking in a low, practiced voice she said, "Her light's still on."

Rebecca nodded. "I know. But I listened at her door and I heard her snoring."

Iris frowned. "I didn't know Aunt Emma snored."

"That doesn't matter now. We have to hurry before it's too late."

Suddenly a door shut downstairs. Both girls slammed their backs against the wall, grabbing each other before they leaped into the bedroom.

"What was that?" Rebecca ran across the room where she carefully stood to the side of the window. She peaked out into the darkness. "I don't see anyone."

"Father must have heard us," Iris informed her. "He was probably checking to see if we were listening outside the door."

Both girls sat on the bed waiting, their eyes fixed on the bedroom door. After a moment, when no one appeared they both dropped their shoulders and sighed in relief.

"I think someone went outside," Rebecca said as she crept back to the window to inspect.

Iris was close behind her, looking over her shoulder into the yard that was dimly lit by a scant moon. Neither girl saw any movement or heard any voices below the half open window.

Iris stepped back into the room. "I think the wind must have caught the kitchen door and slammed it shut. Sometimes Katie forgets to shut it all the way when she leaves."

Rebecca turned around, her hand still clinging to the window frame. "But I heard footsteps downstairs."

"It was probably father, or Mr. Branson. They're still down there arguing."

"We'd better hurry before it's too late."

Clinging to one another for reassurance, the girls crept out of the bedroom and down the stairs, stopping momentarily on each step to listen for Aunt Emma when, in fact all they could hear were gruff voices coming from inside the parlor. They stealthily tiptoed across the cold flagstone entry. Iris led Rebecca through the kitchen where they flew out the back door.

Drawing her wrap closer Iris turned to Rebecca. "Stay here. Hide over there in the corner, beside the lilac bush. Don't come out unless you see someone. Then hurry as fast as you can over to the parlor window."

Rebecca nodded rapidly then slipped into the dark corner where she huddled down low. Iris, moving with exaggerated caution disappeared around the corner of the house.

CHAPTER FOUR

By nine o'clock Leo Branson was tired of listening to those two old coots arguing about what happened sixteen years ago. He finally excused himself.

"Think I'll go outside for a smoke," he said, rising from his chair at a slothful pace.

If it was up to him he'd handle it in a quick and easy way. He'd plead self defense and then pay his solicitor a profitable visit where he'd have a contract written up to prove that Stratton had agreed to the marriage years ago. Then that prissy little snip who acted like she was a notch above everyone else wouldn't have a word to stand on when it came time for him to take what should, by all rights, belong to him.

Leo struck a match on the heel of his boot then bent into his clumsily rolled cigarette, taking a couple of long drags before his head came up. He exhaled, and then looked squint-eyed around the yard. He could have sworn that he heard voices. They were probably coming from one of the upstairs windows. No doubt that old biddy of an aunt reminding her niece of how she's too proper for the likes of him. For a moment he wondered what he was doing out here, standing in the dark thinking up ways to trap a woman into marrying him. He didn't need Stratton's uppity daughter who would no doubt prove to be as lifeless as the rail he was leaning against. He could go into town anytime it suited him and pick up a gal who appreciated his charm and wit. If it wasn't for the land, and the fact that in time he'd gain access to Stratton's money that's exactly where he would be instead of tipping tea cups in some cramped parlor.

He took another long puff from his cigarette then tipped his bristled chin up into the slight breeze that rustled...wait, that wasn't the sound of wind in the trees. Someone was out there moving around...and he was about to find out who.

Leo walked slowly away from the barn. When he was half way across the yard he stopped to listen for any sound of movement. Something was rustling in the grass near the side of the house. Probably nothing but a cat chasing after a mouse. He took one last draw on the stub between his forefinger and thumb then flicked the lighted butt to the ground, mashing it with the tip of his boot before he started toward the house.

As he drew nearer something told him that whatever was prowling around had to be bigger than a cat. Drawing his coat aside he reached inside his waistband and pulled out a derringer. Adrenalin began to pump rapidly through his body. He could feel his heart hammering against his ribs. Maybe the night wouldn't be a total waste after all.

...

Iris shivered. Even with her hands tucked tightly under her arms she was freezing. She forgot how cold it could be outside in the middle of the night with the wind blowing straight across the prairie. In her haste she'd forgotten to put on her slippers and now her feet felt like ice. She teetered on one foot, holding the other under her gown against her leg until it was warm, or until she lost her balance. Then she switched feet. Maybe this wasn't such a good idea after all. She could barely hear what her father and Mr. Branson were saying, only catching a word or two that didn't make any sense on its own. She'd stand a better chance of figuring out what they were talking about if she was eavesdropping at the top of the stairs, and inside she wouldn't run the risk of catching a cold. The thought no sooner left her when she heard a movement behind her. Thinking that it was Rebecca she quickly turned around when all at once a large hand flew across her face. She screamed while fighting against the strong arm that encircled her. But her cries remained trapped inside her throat.

"Well, look at what I found out here in the dark. A peeping Tom."

Leo Branson's lecherous voice roughly sought Iris' ear while Iris kicked and clawed like a wild cat until Leo roughly turned her around to face him. The gun still in his hand, he pinned her back against the side of the house. Bending over until his piercing eyes met hers he jeered. "Ya' really think yer somethin', don't ya', Girlie? You, with yer nose in the air, snubbin' me all the time we're sittin' in your little tea room. Well, let me tell ya' somethin', Missy." He put his face so close to Iris' that the strong smell of tobacco made her gag. "It's time someone took ya' down a notch or two."

Iris tried to squirm out of Leo's hold, her screams muffled by his hand that remained clamped over her mouth. She could no longer hear voices from inside the house and prayed that her father had somehow discovered that she was gone and would come looking for her.

Leo grabbed a fist full of her hair and turned her head until their faces met. His grizzled jaw moved toward her and she jerked her head to the side, which only made it easier for his lips to touch her ear while he threatened her.

"One of these days I'm goin' ta take the starch right outta yer high and mighty attitude ya' flaunt so prettily. Until then I don't need yer kind. There's others more willin' than you."

The front door slammed shut and Leonard Branson could be heard shouting across the yard. "Ya' won't get away with this Stratton. I'm gonna make you sorry that you ever knew me. Leo! Come on, let's go."

Iris fought against the boards that cut into her back. Where was Rebecca?

"Looks like the party's over for now. It's been a real pleasure chattin' with ya'. I'm sure you feel the same way," Leo sneered. "You just keep one thing in mind, Girlie. I always get what I want, so you can bet I'll be back, cause yor mine. Ya' hear me?"

Iris saw a flash of white to the side of Leo's shoulder and suddenly Rebecca was charging at his back. There was a loud crack followed by Rebecca's stifled cry. Leo let out a painful groan and dropped his hold on Iris, grabbing his shoulder. Iris didn't know what possessed her. She should have run as fast as she could but instead she flew to the ground, clambering for the piece of board that Rebecca used to hit Leo. Iris shot up and swung at him, striking him across the back until he barreled around and grabbed the other end of the board with a grip so strong that it whipped Iris right off her feet. Frantically she fought the fullness of her gown until she had it bunched in her hands and was able to get up. Turning sharply she darted across the yard where she ran headlong into Rebecca. The two of them tumbled to the ground. Iris fell back on her hands, letting out a desperate cry when she looked up and saw through the moonlight Leo lumbering toward them.

"Rebecca! Run!" She shouted frantically while both girls fought to get to their feet again.

"Leo! Come on. Let's get outta here." Leonard's angry voice penetrated the night.

The girls staggered to their feet, clinging to each other, their eyes wide with fright when Leo, who was panting heavily, stopped short in front of them. He leered down at Iris, lifting her chin with the barrel of his derringer.

"Yer little friend ain't gonna be around to save ya' next time."

He drew his shirt sleeve across his beaded forehead while his livid eyes matched the cold blue of Iris' glare. He shoved the pistol back into his waistband and staggered away.

Iris and Rebecca waited until they could no longer hear the sound of the departing wagon. Then, hand in hand, they ran swiftly to the back door. Iris cracked the door open, listening carefully for sounds from inside the house. After a moment of quiet she slipped into the warm kitchen, with Rebecca clinging to her back. She quickly shut the door, locking it before she fell back and caught her breath. At last they were safe. All at once she turned and looked sharply at Rebecca.

"I don't know why I let you talk me into going out there. I couldn't hear a thing they were saying," She paused. "And Leo Branson nearly killed me with his filthy hand over my mouth smothering the life out of me."

Iris stormed across the room, headed upstairs, and

Rebecca scurried after her. "How was I supposed to know that he was out there?" Light-footed, Iris started up the steps before Rebecca thought to add, "You thought it was a good idea before he showed up."

Iris turned abruptly, colliding into Rebecca who grabbed the banister to keep herself from toppling over. "And I nearly froze to death. See!" She swiftly touched the side of Rebecca's neck with her frigid fingers and Rebecca squealed, scrunching up her shoulders.

Iris' hand clamped over Rebecca's mouth while her eyes quickly darted toward the light that still lined the floor under her aunt's bedroom door. "Shh! You'll wake up Aunt Emma."

Without moving her head Rebecca looked at the door. When the door didn't open Iris slowly pulled her hand away, sighing through parted lips.

"We have to hurry and pin up your hem. If we don't get it done, Aunt Emma will ask me what we've been doing all night."

Once inside the bedroom Rebecca hurried into her dress then stood on a chair. With a certain amount of skill and agility Iris had the hem pinned up and basted in half an hour.

"That'll have to do," she said, poking the remaining pins into the velvet pin cushion.

"Right now I'm too tired to care what the hem looks like," Rebecca said as she climbed out of her dress, laying it across the foot of the bed. She slipped her nightgown over her head and crawled into the bed, curling into the down quilt and feather pillow. By the time Iris combed her hair and braided it Rebecca was asleep.

...

Iris turned down the wick in the lamp then carried it across the room and set it on the bedside table. For once she was glad that Rebecca had fallen asleep early. Since the dilemma in the parlor she hadn't even had a minute to herself to think about Andrew. He had to be the one building the corral over at the Stevens' place. He was John Stevens closest friend, the only one, from what Iris could gather, that John had ever brought home from college. How wonderful it would be if it was true. Going back to her dressing table she picked up her book of poetry and her trinket box then walked around to the other side of the bed where she drew back the quilt and climbed in beside Rebecca. She leaned back into her pillow then opened the book of poetry and picked up the dried violets. Putting them to her nose she closed her eyes and breathed deeply, pretending that the scent was as strong as it was the day Andrew gave them to her. Replacing the flowers, she withdrew a blue ribbon, the same one that she had used to hold back her hair on that day with Andrew. Now she tied the ribbon at the end of her braid, then reached inside her trinket box and took out a man's worn leather glove. She held it briefly to the side of her face thinking how much it smelled like gunpowder and horses running through the wind, things that reminded her of Andrew. She wondered if he was in the habit of losing things as she laid the glove back inside the box and withdrew a black button. She remembered finding it in the grass several days after Andrew had gone back to Boston.

Andrew Burgess had come to spend a few months with John Stevens on John's father's farm, a few miles down the road from the Strattons. Iris had never seen much of John while growing up. He was eight years older than she and had left at an early age, after his mother had died, to live with his aunt in Boston, where he attended school. Over the years Iris had heard much about John, since their fathers had been friends for a long time. There were times, when he had been home for a few weeks in the summer when she had caught a glimpse of him. It was usually when he had been out riding, or in town in the Merchantile, where she had hidden behind stacked shelves and watched him.

It was last summer, just after she had turned fifteen. On that particularly hot day, while she had been out riding, she saw Andrew rounding up some stray calves. She had thought she was hidden well by a stand of trees and had decided to nudge her horse closer in order to get a better look at the stranger. He sat taller in his saddle than she had ever seen any man sit, and his wide shoulders fell in a straight line down the expanse of his back. His legs were so long he seemed almost too big for his horse, though the mount made a perfect picture. It had been impossible to see what his face looked like with the brim of his Stetson pulled down over his forehead, but she didn't care at the time. She had decided to wait and save that for another day.

She remembered leaning into Honey's neck, hoping to get a closer look at the man when all at once she saw him pull out his pistol. Then with a tight grip on his reins he had started charging toward the trees after her. Iris had panicked and whipped her horse around. She'd galloped as fast as she could down Stoney Creek Road toward home. She had never been chased by a man on horseback before, nor had she ever flown through the wind as fast as Honey had taken her. Feeling exhilarated and scared at the same time, she had jabbed Honey's sides and shouted, "Yeehaw", holding onto the reins so tight that her hands had ached for days. A shot had suddenly rung through the air. Iris now remembered the burning pain and the sound of her own scream just before she had gone flying out of her saddle into the ravine. Later, she had been told that when Andrew discovered she was a girl, and not a rustler, and that his bullet had clipped her shoulder, he went wild with regret. When he had checked under the flap on her saddle he saw her initials and the Stratton brand. With Iris secure in his arms he had swiftly mounted his horse then flew down the length of Stoney Creek Road to the Stratton farm. When he reached the house he had kicked the door open and strode inside, shouting for help. Iris didn't have to be told what had happened after that. When her father found out that one of Stevens' men had shot his daughter he'd grabbed his rifle and would have shot Andrew right where he stood if Aunt Emma hadn't fought him back. By then Iris had regained consciousness. It had taken every ounce of energy she'd had to convince her father that she was all right and that the shooting had been an accident.

Going against his own judgment, Edward had decided

not to shoot Andrew but instead sternly warned him not to come back...since he never knew when he might change his mind. By that time Iris was smitten. She had never seen a man as handsome as Andrew Burgess, or one so reckless. The light that had come through the window had reflected off hair the color of the sun in autumn, a firm unshaven jaw, and eyes that had flashed a ready smile that had headed straight for her heart.

The next day Andrew had sent flowers and the day after that he sent candy that the Stevens' cook had made special for the occasion. By the third day he hadn't been able to stay away any longer and so took his chances. He delivered the book of Tennyson poems himself.

Iris had been sitting in a wicker chair under a tree with a glass of lemonade in her hand when she saw Andrew ride into the yard. With a hand near her brow, to keep the flickering sunlight out of her eyes, she had greeted him softly. Words could never describe the sensation that had whirled through her body when he dismounted, walked over to where she was sitting and sat down in the grass beside her. He had leaned back against the tree with one long leg outstretched and the other bent close to his chest, his wrists crossed on his knee. Without having been asked to do so, Andrew had taken off his hat, ran his tanned fingers through hair that looked like a mass of tangled sunbeams and began to talk. They had spent the entire afternoon, sitting in the dappled shade, a gentle breeze mingling their words softly together.

"You're not by any chance related to the Stratton's from Boston, are you?" Andrew had inquired.

"As a matter of fact, I am," Iris had replied with confidence. "My Grandfather was John Stratton..."

"You mean the founder of the largest import-export business in Boston?" Andrew had interrupted.

Iris nodded briefly before she had explained further. "He came to America from Germany in 1808, as a stow-a-way. He had stumbled upon another stow-a-way, a gentleman disguised as a vagrant. It has been told that this man had threatened to kill my Grandfather if he revealed his presence. My Grandfather was young and alone, so he befriended the man, sneaking food for both of them."

"Did they start a business together after arriving in Boston?" Andrew had asked with interest.

Iris then shook her head. "The man was a thief."

"Did he say as much?" Andrew had frowned in what had appeared to be concern.

"No." Iris had glanced up at the house before she continued. "There was a terrible storm that lasted for several days. The man became deathly ill. Just before he died he gave my grandfather a bag of gold. He told him to make a life for himself in America."

Andrew had nodded with a calculated look on his face. "He starts a business that proves successful, then slips into society where he's then sought after by every available debutante."

"It's like a fairy tale," Iris had said, smiling. "Soon after he arrived in America he married Eleanor Calvert. A year later my father was born. He grew up in Boston where he met my mother, Lydia Rutledge."

She specifically remembered Andrew having said, "You come from some well known and respected Boston families, Miss Stratton."

"I suppose that's important if one lives in Boston, but out here, a man makes his own name." She had answered with confidence.

"Humph," Andrew had mused. "And so, how does Nebraska fit into the story?"

"Well, father left Boston when he was twenty-one to start a new life. His mother died a short time after that, but father didn't go back to Boston until his father died. That's when he met mother and proposed marriage. Unfortunately, her parents objected."

"Realizing who your father's family was they must have later changed their mind," Andrew had speculated.

"To the contrary," Iris expounded, with cheeks flushed from the excitement of telling the story. "They had adamantly refused to grant mother permission to marry a farmer, which is what father wanted to become. So, my father and mother eloped."

"Thereby ending all family connections and any ties with Boston society," Andrew had concluded.

"I never thought of it as a sacrifice, but you're right. Mother was no doubt disowned. No one mentions her side of the family, and I've never seen any pictures of them. They must have written after Mother died, but I've never been told about a letter."

"I'm sorry...about your mother," Andrew had spoken softly.

"It's all right. I never knew her. I've always thought of Aunt Emma as my real mother." Iris had taken a deep breath as she'd glanced up at Andrew. "I'm sure you have just as interesting a background, Mr. Burgess."

"I'm afraid it's not nearly as intriguing as yours," Andrew had begun. "No stow-a-ways or ancestors falling into great fortune. My mother is a woman of society and my father is a ship builder. I worked in the ship yard myself until I went to college. That's where I met John Stevens. It was his love of horses and adventure that brought me to Nebraska." They both had smiled then, each secretly happy with the choice he'd made.

The afternoon had passed swiftly with Iris explaining all the many activities to look forward to now that winter was over. Andrew had left before Iris' father came home and later Iris found the button, the button that, since that day, she held to her lips every night before going to bed. Rebecca had once told her that she was wasting her time dreaming about a man who was still going to college in Boston. But how could Iris ever forget him? How could she erase the picture of him lying at her feet reciting poetry? He had never told her that he loved her, but before he went away he kissed her goodbye.

Time had passed and he never wrote. There had been word of him only when she rode over to the Stevens with her father and

Mr. Stevens happened to mention John and Hawk and their friend, Andrew. She had never expected to see him again.

But now he was back.

Iris kissed the button, whispering, "If I can't have you then I don't want anyone. I'll always be here, Andrew...waiting for you."

CHAPTER FIVE

As soon as Andrew Burgess arrived in Nebraska he was put to work hauling material for a corral in a wagon that Jacob Stevens had waiting for him at the depot. Every day since then, he was up at dawn and to bed as soon as the last blanket of darkness spread itself over the prairie, the same wide, windy prairie that kept distracting him, forcing him to raise his head and look down the length of Stoney Creek Road toward the Stratton farm. He frowned, wondering what had come over him the past few days. He'd no sooner start a task than unbidden thoughts of what had happened last summer started crowding in on him, causing him to lose track of what he was doing. He once traveled all over Europe where he'd seen spectacular plays and mystifying magic shows, but they were nothing when compared to the magic act that soared through his body every time he thought about Iris Stratton. He kept seeing her face in his mind, the image so vivid it was as though she were standing right there in front of him. He remembered last summer sitting in the grass at her feet, the way her shoulder flounced when she bent her head to look down at him. Her lavender eyes sparkled in the sunlight slipping through the leafy boughs and glancing off her hair, a billowing mass of midnight sky held away from her rosy cheeks by a strip of blue ribbon. The image left him feeling weak. He set down his hatchet and stretched his back muscles. The windlass creaked and Andrew turned his head toward the lonely sound. He never remembered ever feeling lonely until that hot summer day when he rode away from the Stratton farm.

Beyond the giant windmill there was land as far as he could see, rich furrowed soil just beginning to offer itself to the whispering touch of spring. At first he thought it was the land that made him want to come back. But now he knew that it was Iris, and Iris was a part of the land.

He took off his hat, and then pulling off his bandana he tied it around his forehead, anticipating a long hot day as he studied the grey skyline above a row of swaying cottonwoods. The prairie was forever a new and mysterious place. It did strange things to a man. He never told Iris that he loved her, but the feeling never left him. She seemed to care for him though she had never said as much. He no doubt mistook her kindly manner for affection, so he never wrote. He didn't want to take advantage of the situation. After all he did shoot her. The thought still made him wince. Should he come across too strongly after that she might feel obligated to be kind to him. Besides, at the time he wasn't sure if he was ever going to make it back this way. That's when he concluded that love was like this swelling grassland.

John Stevens once told him that this land could be as tender as a first kiss or as violent as a raging bull. The strangest thing of all was how one minute a man could be passionately in love with its beauty and goodness, then in the time it took him to turn one furrow with a plow the sky could be transformed, from endless blue to a front of dark clouds goaded on by fierce winds. The sudden change filled his heart with traitorous blasphemies, and for a time he despised the land's unrelenting fury and reckless will. While Andrew had never personally experienced the anger of the plains he grew fascinated at the prospect of owning a piece of this unpredictable earth.

While back in Boston he often dreamed of the endless possibilities that Nebraska had to offer. He remembered the first time he rode across the expanse of the prairie. He knew then, in the seconds that it took him to absorb its greatness, that this was where he wanted to be.

Andrew's eyes shifted momentarily toward the hen house where the hens were just beginning to stir. He wondered if most men felt the way he had when they first saw wide open places. He concluded that they must either love the land or hate it. There was no time in between for wondering if someday you could become a part of it, or if it would become a part of you. The feeling was either there inside of you at the start or it wasn't.

He shook his head, then positioned his hat before he

picked up his hatchet. He carved out another notch then set the hatchet down and hoisted a split rail, fitting both ends tight before he used the butt end of the hatchet to hammer the rail firmly in place. The thudding sound echoed in the emptiness surrounding him. What was he doing out here day dreaming like a school boy? Before he knew it more than one hundred and fifty head of horses would be moving this way, and the corral better be done because there was no way in hell he was going to miss the chance to be right in the middle of the drive. He'd give his right arm rather than pass up the overwhelming feeling of exhilaration that was already beginning to shoot through his veins at the mere thought of the sound of thundering horse flesh carving a swath as wide as a canyon across the middle of Nebraska.

The screen door up at the house flapped shut and Andrew looked up to see Ida, the Stevens' housekeeper walking steadily toward him with a tin cup in her hand. It was plain enough to see that Indian blood had slipped into her family line. Her hair, that was long and black, had a touch of grey in it, and her swarthy skin delicately spanned her high cheek bones. She hadn't said much to him since he'd arrived, but she made up for it by always being around whenever he was hungry or thirsty. He stopped working and reached for the cup of water that he drank in one long gulp.

"If you drink fast in the heat you get sick," Ida said without expression.

Andrew drew the back of his hand across his mouth. "Thanks for telling me."

"You don't work tomorrow," she added, changing the subject abruptly. "There's a picnic at the Strattons'. Then at night they all dance."

Andrew handed the cup back to Ida. "You're going to dance aren't you?" he coaxed teasingly.

Ida quickly shook her head and Andrew wondered if she turned and walked away because she was blushing. "Dancing is for young people," she replied over her shoulder.

Andrew watched her walk back to the house. He'd never

seen such a mixture of people as he'd seen while heading west. For a moment he set his mind to daydreaming again, wondering about the wagon trains, thinking about budding romances going on between people of all sorts of backgrounds and races. It was strange how a country came to be. It all...he'd never get another post set if he didn't stop his dallying.

He drove the post hole digger into the soft fertile soil turning the handle until the tongs were full of dirt, which he deposited off to the side. He hadn't been to a picnic in years, but he sure liked to dance. He gave the corral a quick once over. Actually he was making good progress. He wouldn't feel too bad about taking a day off.

Besides, Iris would be there. Since he hadn't written, he wondered what he should say to her, if her father would even let him near enough to say anything? He hoped Edward Stratton wasn't still carrying a grudge because Andrew had mistaken his daughter for a rustler. What was he supposed to have thought? There'd been talk of cattle thieves in the area and she was hiding back in the trees with her hair up under a hat and wearing a ridiculous pair of men's britches and a baggy shirt, unlike what most ladies wore. He just assumed that she was a rustler keeping a close eye on the Stevens' cattle. Dang it all! If that wasn't the worst day of his life; he hoped to God he wouldn't live long enough to see it. He had shot a woman!

CHAPTER SIX

Emma woke up at dawn when she heard someone creeping down the stairs. The back door creaked open then padded shut. She went to the window and through the curtain made of Brussels lace she saw Rebecca run across the yard then down the road toward home. Whenever Rebecca stayed the night she always left early in the morning to help her brother milk the cows. Emma pulled on her wrapper. Gathering the front under her chin with one hand she sat down on the wine and pink flowered cushion on the window seat, drawing her feet up under her body to keep them warm. She propped her elbows on the sill and, resting her chin in her hands she watched the sun come up.

Emma was glad that Iris had Rebecca for a friend. She always hoped that Rebecca's fondness for cooking and gardening, not to mention dressmaking would influence Iris to take more interest in homemaking. Instead, Iris continued to spend most of her time outdoors riding horses while wearing her father's trousers, or lying in the prairie grass picking wildflowers and reading poetry. Emma frowned, wondering if she had been too hard on Iris over the years. She closed her eyes for a lingering moment, her lips pursed tightly together before she shook her head, having quickly concluded that it just wasn't so. Someone had to keep that girl in line. Edward knew nothing about raising children, especially a girl; and, even though Emma had never had a child of her own, she was more of a mother to Iris than Lydia had ever been.

Slightly parting the curtain, Emma craned her neck to look at the rose garden just below the window. A hint of faint sunlight touched her face and she turned her lashes down. The pink roses were just beginning to open. Up close they looked like a baby's mouth set in a delicate yawn, all pink and white and soft. Years ago Edward discovered the roses growing wild near a stream and had transplanted them for his young bride. But Emma had long ago stopped thinking of the garden as belonging to Lydia. It was her garden now. The same way that Iris was now hers.

If fate was to blame and there was no way to alter the past then Emma was glad that Edward had sent for her when Iris was a baby. When still a young woman about to be married, Emma was forced to choose between the pursuit of marriage to Silas, a man of prominence in Boston or coming to Nebraska to care for Iris. Emma knew now that she had made the right choice. Iris was the baby that she would never have had if she had married. When she was a child she fell off of her pony while jumping hurdles. Her foot had become ensnared in the stirrup and the horse dragged her across the yard and through the underbrush in a small wooded area nearby. By the time her father was able to stop the horse she was unconscious and badly bruised. A few weeks later the doctor informed her parents that she would never be able to bare children. As it turned out a few months after Emma went to live with Edward and Iris, Silas married the woman who had turned down his proposal of marriage only a few months before he had met Emma. Any tenderness left in Emma's heart quickly vanished. Had Silas merely taken pity on her, willing to marry her rather than go through his life feeling jilted? A short time after Emma arrived at her brother's house none of that seemed to matter. The bitterness she harbored began to fade as her love for Iris grew.

The sun was a bronze circle just above the horizon when Emma let go of the curtain. She could hear someone walking around downstairs and she assumed that is was Stella starting breakfast. Emma was usually dressed by now and in the kitchen planning the day's activities. But the previous night's argument between Edward and the Bransons upset her more than she was at first willing to admit. After she had gone to her room last night she threw back her round floral rug then got down on the floor and put her ear flat against the floor boards. At first she had felt foolish, like a school girl caught eavesdropping in the cloak room, but the feeling quickly vanished when, from what little she heard of the spiraling argument, she became convinced that the proposed marriage would be a grave mistake.

Emma got up and was untying her wrap when she noticed

some dried leaves on the geraniums sitting on a small table near the window. She carefully plucked them off, while cooing over the coral buds. Reaching for the watering can she decided to ride over to the Archers to give a potted plant to Rebecca's mother who was close to having her fifth baby. Beth was only thirty three years old. Emma's thoughts mingled with the blurping sound of the water streaming from the spout. Emma was twenty-one years old when she left Boston to come to Nebraska. She wondered how many children she would have had by now, if it were possible, and she had married at sixteen, like Beth. Her coming here seemed ages ago when she considered how Edward now wanted Iris to start accepting gentleman callers. Her heart swelled, her nose tingling with the urge to cry. She shuddered, quickly squelching feelings of jealousy, but they refused to be squelched. She was now thirty-seven, and in all those years she had never had a gentleman caller. Never a bouquet of wildflowers or a simple kiss good night. A man's fingertips would never caress her face, where her own hand now rested. At times she wondered if her feelings of longing, that she so often pushed aside, would ever find their way into a man's heart. She considered the possibility for a thrilling moment, then wondering what had come over her she resignedly turned back to the window where she could hear Katie beating a rug on the clothes line near the potting shed. She was thinking about calling out the window for Katie to bring in a pot from the shed when she saw Edward walking along the foot path with his easel and a sketch pad in his hand. He was no doubt headed toward the meadow where he painted wildflowers every spring. She watched his long stride leading him away from his cares to a place where he was most happy. Edward was still a strikingly handsome man. Tall and broad shouldered, he carried himself well. His black hair, slightly laced with gray accentuated his dark eyes that Emma was certain could still melt a woman's heart. His firm, smooth shaven face and strong jaw were well defined, a profile he would do well in sketching. If only Edward would stop punishing himself for having brought Lydia to Nebraska, then Emma was sure he would re-marry someday. Just then she noticed the way his hand swung loosely at his side. She wondered if Stella forgot to pack a lunch for him. She frowned, drawing her lips tightly together. Sixteen years of nurturing had forced her to worry overmuch at times, no matter how hard she tried to stop. He would come home when he got hungry. Sweeping aside her frets she took off her wrap then started to get dressed. It wouldn't do her a bit of good to stay in her room half the morning worrying about things that usually took care of themselves.

As with every morning Emma brushed out her long hair, then coiled it and pinned it in its comfortable, familiar place at the nape of her neck. She smiled faintly at her reflection in the mirror. Her hair had kept most of its auburn color, with only an occasional strand of gray that wouldn't be missed after she plucked it out. Methodically she began to dress. She studied her figure in the glass, deciding that lack of childbearing had at least left her with somewhat of a shapely form. She suddenly frowned, recalling how unlady-like she had been last night when upon hearing the girls moving around in the hall she feigned sleep, snoring like a man. She laughed softly, shrugging then began buttoning up her white blouse. What else should she have done? Her light was still on and she didn't feel like answering any questions Iris might be inclined to ask should she decide to knock on the door. Emma's lips formed a straight line, her brows raised in thought. Iris was determined to find out what her father and Mr. Branson were talking about. Emma could hardly blame her. There had been too many unanswered questions over the years.

Emma slipped a dark blue skirt made of nainsook over her head. She never minded raising Iris but there was one thing she refused to do and that was tell Iris about her mother; it was not her place to do so. With her open hands she brushed the wrinkles down the front of her full skirt then pinned a broach on her high collar. After taking a quick glance around the room she picked up a small clay pot of newly transplanted red geraniums and started downstairs.

...

There was nothing like the song of a bird in spring to set a young boy's heart to fluttering and his mind reeling toward adventure, or to cause a grown man's spirit to become restless. If there was one thing that Edward would never grow tired of it was listening to the melodious call of a meadow lark. It was not only exhilarating it was life sustaining. Whenever he felt down, like he did the minute he opened his eyes that morning, the only thing that could revive him was being outdoors. Once he was sitting on a hillside in the swaying prairie grass with the feel of warm sunshine on his back, nothing could stop him from sketching or dabbing at one of his water colors while listening to the songs of birds as they targeted the wind.

Trudging up the hillside Edward felt himself growing weary and he stopped a minute to catch his breath. It wasn't like him to become so upset over a man's loud, empty threats. He was probably just overly tired. He felt like he hadn't slept a wink all night. He had stayed awake for hours trying to read by the dim light of the lamp when in fact all he did was worry about what Leonard Branson would do now that Leo's proposal had been turned down. Edward had never known Leonard to be so belligerent or unreasonable. His angry claim that Edward had years ago agreed to the marriage of their children was preposterous, his abusive threats bordering on blackmail.

Sixteen years ago Leonard Branson had underhandedly taken advantage of Edward's desperate situation by offhandedly suggesting the possibility of their children someday marrying. Leonard's covert plan was to join their properties which would result in his becoming a wealthy man.

Edward sighed heavily. He didn't come out here to think about Leonard Branson. As soon as he wrote to inform his solicitor of what was said last night he would forget that the matter was ever discussed with the Bransons.

For quite some time Edward studied the sky. The clouds overhead were huge and downy white, even more so when cast against a powdery blue background. He took a deep breath then exhaled. He loved being a water colorist, especially in the spring when everything around him was new, lying there waiting to be stroked, like a beautiful woman. He started walking again. No, he would never forget how beautiful a woman could be. He thought about his painting of Lydia, the one that still hung in the oval frame in his bedroom. Though it was one of his best works it didn't do her justice. Lydia's flawless skin was as white as a magnolia blossom, her cheeks the faint color of a rose, something few artists could perfect. Her eyes were a vivid pastel blue with black lashes that fanned her cheeks like a delicate fern. Her striking ebony hair was pinned up in back. Curls nestled across her brow, just beneath the brim of her weaved hat, laden with roses and tied down with a silk bow. Her slender neck, accentuating her delicately sloping shoulders, was enveloped in a lace collar where a broach was fastened, an heirloom that once belonged to Lydia's great grandmother. Everything about the painting displayed Lydia's gentle upbringing.

Edward stopped at his favorite spot on the hillside overlooking a meadow where occasionally the cattle grazed. Today they were lazing by the pond near a grove of leafy trees. He sat down on the wooden chair that was always there, waiting faithfully for him. Positioning his easel, he laid his sketch pad on it, moving it this way and that until the unsuspecting scene lay perfectly in view. He thought how nice it would be to sketch Iris standing with her parasol in a breezy patch of wildflowers. He once painted her mother sitting on a patch quilt in the sunshine with crocus dotting the grass. His eyes lowered in thought. How could he blame her for what had happened? He was wrong to bring her to this unpredictably harsh place, no matter how much he loved her. He could forgive all her cruel treatment, and in fact he had forgiven her years ago. The only thing he held against her was the lie that she forced him to live. He knew it was wrong to deceive Iris, but Lydia left him no choice. Leaning forward, his hands clasped tightly between his spread knees his jaw clenched for a painful moment. He was never good at explaining his feelings or why things happened the way they did. How could he tell Iris that her mother hated everything that he had given to her?

After Lydia went away, she contacted Edward through her solicitor, informing him that she would never return to Nebraska. She did not wish to obtain a divorce, nor did she want to be contacted, though she expected a monthly allotment be sent through her solicitor. Still Edward sent letters, and at times miniatures of Iris, along with clippings of her hair and her first baby tooth. Having never received a reply he finally gave up correspondence. He stopped quizzing his solicitor as to Lydia's whereabouts. The years passed and eventually he assumed that she had died. That was his story to Iris. At times he regretted harboring the painful truth, but what else could he do? Lydia had left him no other choice. If Emma hadn't been there to console him, and to be a mother to Iris he would have gone mad.

A scented breeze brushed over him. He closed his eyes with his face turned up into the sun. He rocked from side to side gently absorbing the serene feeling that overtook him. He couldn't complain. Life had given him a measure of happiness. He was grateful for that. Though he was lonely at times, he was content to live out the rest of his days here on the prairie, on the land that he loved.

...

An hour later, after realizing that she had missed breakfast, Iris lifted the curtain at her bedroom window. In the distance she could barely see her father sitting on the hillside pouring his feelings onto a canvas. Aunt Emma was just leaving the yard in the buggy, heading down the road toward Beth Archer's house, her arms held straight out in front of her as she guided the reins. With her head held high, her eyes fixed on the road and her shoulders held respectfully back like a school marm's, Iris watched as her aunt set about her day's activities. There was a basket of food and a pot of red geraniums on the seat beside her. Iris dropped the curtain, smiling at her aunt who was most content when she was giving to others. A person could almost see her heart swelling with gratitude. How many times had Aunt Emma said, 'words couldn't describe how good it felt to be needed?'

Hurriedly dressing, Iris cast aside fleeting thoughts concerning the previous night's activities and set her mind on the task of baking a cake for the raffle that was to be held by the school board at the picnic the following day. She had never made a cake before but it couldn't be that hard. Anyone could read a recipe.

Iris wasn't in the kitchen more than fifteen minutes before clouds of flour were wafting through the air and she was apologizing to Stella, the Stratton's German cook, for the egg that slipped from her wet fingers and splattered onto the floor. Stella shuffled, all in a tizzy, from one side of the kitchen, where she grabbed a rag, to the other side, where in seconds she was on her hands and knees wiping up the runny egg and bits of shell. When she looked up to scold Iris for being so messy a dollop of batter flew from the spoon in Iris' hand and landed just above Stella's right eye. She made a grumbling noise inside her throat as she gripped the edge of the table and pulled her ample body up off the floor. Then like a hen being chased by a cat Stella fluttered over to the sink waving her spread hands out in front of her, squawking, "<u>Menschens Kind</u>! <u>Menschens Kind</u>!" There was a brief truce, when she remained across the room watching Iris who was studiously bent at the waist pondering over the order in which to add the remaining ingredients. Iris swept her hand over the page that was spattered with clumps of butter and dustings of flour. Reaching for another egg, she cracked it. Then, just as the egg was sliding down the mound of flour she cried out, "Ohh! Does it matter if there are a few little pieces of the shell in it?"

"Ja!" Stella was at the table in three quick steps, her hands raised above her shaking head. "Give me dat bowl." She reached out to grab the bowl and wooden spoon from Iris who backed away shaking her head adamantly.

"No! This is my cake." Iris insisted. "I'm making it for

someone special."

"He von't be somevone special after he eats dat cake." Stella warned, her hands on her stout hips, her elbows jutting out like the handles on a sugar bowl. "He'll be somevone seek."

Iris frowned, pursing her lips the way Aunt Emma did when she wanted Iris to know that she was displeased with her. Iris continued to flip the spoon in a circular motion, her head bobbing from side to side with the thudding rhythm the spoon made against the crock bowl. "Look." Iris slanted the bowl until the batter was dangerously near the rim. "It looks just like your batter."

Plop! A spoonful of the lumpy batter landed on the flowered oil cloth covering the table then careened over the edge where it landed on the floor with the egg swirled blotches of flour dust. Disgusted with the whole business, Stella shoved the baking pans across the table, her stern expression insisting that the cake was ready to put into the oven. After Iris reluctantly scooped the lumpy batter into the pans, Stella thrust the concoction into the dark gaping hole then slammed the door shut. Turning around sharply, her plump hands held out in front of her she hustled Iris out of the kitchen. Then with arms akimbo and feet apart Stella blocked the doorway, her eyes flashing a warning. "And I don't vant to see you back in here til I make da frosting and clean up da keetchen."

Affronted, Iris tore off her apron, threw back her shoulders and huffed. Stella's expression caused Iris to heave a voluntary sigh. There was no sense arguing the issue when she had so many other things to do before the day was over. She still had to make bows for the platform out of the bunting that Aunt Emma saved after her coming out party. Deciding that she was quite pleased with the morning's achievements she surrendered her apron to Stella then turned and went to search for Aunt Emma.

CHAPTER SEVEN

From the porch, Iris saw Hickory, one of the stable hands, across the yard brushing Aunt Emma's horse. She went back inside the house where she found her aunt in the front parlor sitting at her secretary writing a letter. She inquired after the bunting and her aunt, distracted by her thoughts, cast a quick glance in Iris' direction, then after a moment's silence stated that the bunting was in a straw basket in the attic.

"The attic," Iris muttered, thinking that Aunt Emma usually went to the attic herself if there was something up there that was hard to find. Her brows came together then lifted in compliance as she turned to leave, not wanting to disturb her aunt any longer.

She moved swiftly through the house anxious to get started on the bows. Opening the door to the attic she gripped the sides of her skirt then climbed up the steep narrow steps. When her eyes were level with the floor and she could see, through a dusty shaft of light that poured through a single window, the silhouetted objects in the triangular room, an intrusive feeling came over her. It was the same feeling that she had experienced only once before in her life when she was sent to search through her father's closet for a vest he couldn't find. Then, as now, she felt as though she was going back in time to a place where she didn't belong, and in fact had never even been thought of yet. The air was heavy with unspoken memories and untouched dreams. She wondered for a childish moment, if by touching the objects, she would become linked somehow to the illusion that was her mother.

With one hand she grabbed onto the side of a huge trunk to pull herself up the last step and into the musty room. Then turning around, she sat down on the floor with her skirt filling the stairwell. She sat for a quiet moment studying the cob webbed rafters and the odd images the shadows made, while allowing the feeling of an uncertain past to penetrate her sense of reality. Someday, someone else would be sitting where she was sitting now, perhaps pondering as she was over past events in the lives of people long forsaken.

She reached out and touched an overstuffed pillow with faded pink and mauve roses done in needlepoint, while pretending that her hand was her mother's hand touching the woven threads. Quickly she drew her closed hand back, laying it protectively against her bodice. She didn't know why she thought of her mother just then. In all these years she had only seen a watercolor portrait of her. Perhaps it was because the pillow was there lying on a rumpled piece of quilting for her to touch. A contemplative frown altered her expression. The portrait, like the pillow was lifeless as were the many colorless shapes that ended up in perplexing piles in a room that people seldom entered. Their unintelligible volume offered no comfort, only dark, elongated shadows. She bowed her head, seemingly to study her fingers fidgeting in her lap, and then raised her eyes to a stack of books lying on several odd shaped band boxes covered in wallpaper and balancing precariously on a spindly dark wood table. She bit her lower lip and, drawing her arched brows over her perplexing gaze, wondered if she should continue her mental inspection when a disturbing thought occurred to her. Would her book of Tennyson poems someday be added to those castaways? That would make her as near to her mother as she would ever get. She winced at the thought, never wanting to part with anything that Andrew had touched. Sitting upright her heart swelled with confusion and pain. Why should knowing her mother mean the discarding of her own treasures? She got up, her skirts stirring through the dusty sunbeam and walked over to the table where she picked up three books. Turning them on their sides she read the titles in an undertone. "Poetry by Lord Byron, Selected Works by William Shakespeare, Camelot." She turned back one of the dusty covers and saw a faded name scrawled in black ink. She swished the age from the cover page and whispered, "Lydia Rutledge." She traced the name, sounding out the letters, as her shaky finger glided with her stirring emotions.

She started when Aunt Emma's voice came barreling up

the stairwell. "Iris! Did you find the bunting?"

"Yes! I'm coming." Iris thrust the books on top of the uneven stack then looked hurriedly around searching for the straw basket. When she caught sight of it she hastily made her way through the various shades of grey shadows until she was half way across the attic. It wasn't until she picked up the basket that she noticed it had been sitting on top of a tiny cradle, an exact replica of her own baby cradle that was now in her bedroom displaying her china dolls. Before there was even time to sort through the rush of unexplainable emotions that assailed her she dropped the basket and was bent over touching the ivy carved along the side of the cradle. Her fingers stopped at the tiny crocus that bloomed throughout.

The sound of echoing footsteps in the stairwell whisked away her thoughts. "Iris! Stella wants to know if she should put the icing on your cake."

Iris spun around, her fingers fumbling to pick up the basket. She maneuvered her way toward the opening at the top of the stairs while fighting back the burning sensation that pricked her nose and caused her eyes to become blurred. She sniffed, sure of her composure before she answered. "I guess it's all right. I have so many other things to do."

Her aunt turned around and was headed back down the stairs before Iris started down behind her. "If you weren't dallying in the attic you would have more time to finish your work." Emma mildly scolded.

By the time Iris reached the bottom of the stairs her aunt was headed toward the door carrying her garden gloves and a pair of shears in her hand.

"Aunt Emma?" Iris' voice was filled with uncertainty.

Emma stopped. "What's the matter, Iris?"

Iris raised her head, lowered it, then looked straight into her aunt's questioning eyes. "Why is there another cradle in the attic?"

There was a moment of stunned silence when Iris saw her

aunt's face pale. Emma's mouth pursed, while her hand seemed to tighten on the shears. She caught a deep breath before replying. "Your mother lost a baby before you were born."

"Why didn't anyone ever tell me?" Iris blurted.

"I don't know," Emma said plainly.

"Was it a boy or a girl?" Iris shot back.

"It was a boy," Emma answered in a matter-of-fact tone of voice.

"Didn't father ever talk to you about it?" Iris wondered aloud.

"No, he never spoke about it after it happened."

"But why?" Iris demanded.

Uneasy, Emma replied tersely. "That was none of my business."

"None of your business?" Iris shouted. "I suppose it's none of my business either."

Emma's face darkened. "Don't speak to me in that tone of voice."

Iris was shaking, her eyes burning with tears that she quickly stifled. "I'll ask father then." She started toward the door with her head turned away when Emma reached out and touched her arm to stop her.

"It will only upset him, Iris."

Iris drew her arm back. "What about me? No one ever cares if I'm upset."

"That isn't true, and you know it." Emma took a deep breath to calm herself. Her face softened. "It happened a long time ago Iris. It would only hurt your father to talk about it now." She paused. "Sometimes sad memories are better left buried."

There was a weighty silence between them, each one standing as still as the memory concealed. Then Emma said in a kind, understanding voice, "I was just going outside to cut some flowers for the picnic. Do you want to come along?"

Iris shook her head slightly, forcing herself to look up at her aunt. "I need to finish the bows and then get my dress ready for tomorrow."

Emma reached out and wiped a tear off Iris' flushed cheek. "Be patient dear, someday your father will tell you everything you want to know."

Iris gazed at her aunt as she seemed to open the door in slow motion and walk across the porch then disappear around the side of the house to where the roses were climbing on the rock wall. Iris wondered if her father would ever tell her why there was an 'I' carved on the back of the cradle in the attic identical to the one carved on her cradle.

CHAPTER EIGHT

For the rest of the afternoon Iris avoided everyone in the house. The creative urge to make bows had vanished. She sat outside on a wooden crate mechanically twisting and tying the bunting that no longer appeared colorful or interesting. Her father came out just before supper to hang the lanterns on poles that had been placed at each corner of the platform.

"Supper will be ready soon," he said, hooking a lantern handle over a nail.

Iris lowered her head without commenting. How desperately she wanted to ask him about Mr. Branson's threat and about the cradle with the letter carved in the ivy. Maybe it would upset him, like Aunt Emma had said, but still, she wondered when was the right time for her to ask about her mother?

"What's wrong Iris?" her father paused to look at her. "You've been moping around all day."

Iris simply shook her head while continuing to tack up the bunting. "Nothing. I was just thinking about...about what Mr. Branson said to you."

"That's nothing for you to worry about," Edward reassured her as he made his way around the platform.

Iris sighed. She was tired of unanswered questions. And she wasn't interested in eating. She just wanted to go to bed. The sooner she did the sooner tomorrow would bring Andrew.

But that night sleep escaped her. Lying there staring at the canopy above her bed it occurred to her, just after the clock downstairs struck eleven that Andrew had been at the Stevens' place for nearly a week and not once had he tried to contact her. She sprang upright in the bed, her arms crossed angrily she began talking aloud.

"The least he could've done was send a message. Huh!" She shrugged a shoulder. "Why should he? He never wrote to me, not even once while he was away."

She threw up her hands, cocking her head from side to

side. "If he thinks I'm just going to sit here and hold my breath then he's mistaken."

Iris plopped back down on the bed, burying her face in the comfort of her pillows when she heard the sound of footsteps outside her door. There was a knock and the door slowly opened.

"May I come in?" It was Aunt Emma. Iris decided to ignore her, feigning sleep.

"I'm sorry that you've had such a bad day. I promise tomorrow will be better," Emma whispered around the door.

How could Iris ignore such a promise, or the sincerity in which it was spoken? She rolled over and propped her head up on her pillow.

"Is father angry with me for not coming to supper?" she asked meekly.

"No. But he is concerned about you." Emma stepped into the room pulling the door closed behind her.

Iris sighed heavily. "Aunt Emma? Why didn't you ever get married?"

"Now where did that come from?" Emma crossed the room and Iris watched her white gown swaying in the dark. The bed eased gently when Emma sat down beside her.

Iris stirred under the covers. "I was just wondering."

"Who would have been brave enough to raise you if I had gotten married?"

"Was I really all that bad?" Iris asked in a low voice.

Emma laid her hand on Iris' leg that was curled under the blankets. "You were never bad, Iris. You've just always had an imaginative, carefree spirit, and you needed someone as stubborn as me to help tame it." Emma laughed softly. "Otherwise you would have grown up wearing those britches everyday and running around with your hair flying in a tangled mess, looking like a gypsy."

"It would be fun to be a gypsy," Iris' voice perked up.

"I'm sure," Emma replied. "But then you would be off on some journey down a dusty country road and not at the picnic tomorrow to see your cake won by someone special."

Iris shot up into a sitting position. "Did Stella tell you that?"

"Well, sort of."

Iris' head lowered meekly. "She shouldn't have said anything."

"You know Stella. She can't keep a secret very well." Emma laughed fondly with the back of her fingers lightly touching her lips. Then after a contemplative moment she mused. "I almost got married once; to a man that I thought was very special."

"Did he die?" Iris asked, her eyes wide with curiosity.

"No." Emma paused and Iris feared that her question had caused her aunt to become sad.

"I'm sorry." Iris said, her voice filled with empathy.

Emma patted Iris' leg reassuringly. "It's all right, dear. It all turned out for the better anyway. He married a woman that he loved more than me and I...well, I got to be here with you."

Without saying another word Iris flung her arms around her aunt's neck. "I love you so much," she cried, her wet cheek pressed hard against Emma's face. "I'm sorry that I was such a grouch today."

Emma kissed Iris' cheek. "Tomorrow you'll be too tired to dance if you don't get some sleep."

"I just want you to be happy," Iris pleaded.

Emma reached out and tenderly took hold of Iris' hand. "I am happy, Iris. There's no need to worry about me. I'm just too old to be catching a man's eye, that's all."

Iris shook her head, her fierce words seemed almost practiced, while any previous misgiving regarding Andrew instantly vanished. "But I want you to love someone like I love Andrew."

"And who is Andrew?" Emma inquired.

"Andrew Burgess. He's building the corral over at the Stevens' place. Remember, I met him last summer."

"Oh, that Andrew." Emma's voice grew stern. "If you're

worried about your father being angry you'd better not mention that young man's name around here."

"But Andrew loves me," Iris expounded.

"Has he ever told you that he loves you?" Emma asked in a subdued voice.

Iris' head bent to one side and a tender look captured her eyes. "No, not really." Her eyes lit up. "But I know that he does. He gave me a book of poetry and...And that's why he came back to Nebraska, I'm sure of it."

"You have to be careful, Iris. It wouldn't be proper for a lady to throw herself at a man." Emma cautioned.

"I won't, I promise."

Emma patted Iris' hand. "It's time to go to sleep. It's getting late." She kissed Iris' cheek then stood up and started slowly toward the door.

"Aunt Emma?" Half way across the room Emma turned around when Iris whispered passionately. "I just want a man to think of you when he reads poetry, or when he looks down a long road that seems to go nowhere I want him to see you at the end of that road waiting for him."

Emma placed her hand at her throat and drew her head back. "Goodness, I don't think I've ever had that effect on a man."

"Someday you will," Iris said confidently. Emma declined a reply. Everyone needed to have fanciful notions.

...

Andrew started out for the picnic sometime shortly before noon. Half way down the length of Stoney Creek road, his horse threw a shoe and he was forced to dismount and walk back to the Stevens' farm. All the way back he had a scowl on his face. Things just weren't going as planned. He had pictured himself riding into the Stratton's yard and seeing Iris standing on the spacious wraparound porch watching for him, she being dressed in billowing white with the sunlight glancing off of her glistening black hair. Her violet eyes would be more inviting than the sky in autumn while her plum colored lips would appear softer than a lazy summer afternoon. The way things were turning out he would be late, leaving him little opportunity to explain to Iris why he hadn't sent word that he was back in Nebraska before it was time for the dance to start. He dropped his head to one side, shaking it angrily. Women didn't take kindly to explanations once they were angry. Maybe some flowers would help to patch things up. He stopped near the edge of the gravel road and looked around. Spotting some dandelions he proceeded to gather a handful. They wouldn't look too bad once he added a couple of wildflowers. Walking on, he stopped periodically, picking one flower at a time. Once he had a good size bunch he held them at arms length and, turning his head from side to side, he admired his selection before showing them to Sparky, his horse.

"You think she'll like these?" Andrew asked with what little confidence he could muster up considering that they weren't hot house pansies. The horse nickered softly, tossing his head.

Andrew walked on, carrying the bouquet with his arm bent near his chest. He figured he was the perfect picture of a suitor. Ida had been nice enough to give him a haircut, after which he had splashed water on his head from the pump, then shook off the rest of the spray and added just a touch of Bay Rum that he had brought back from Europe. After combing his hair, he slicked it back with brilliantine before he positioned his Stetson at just the right angle. He had spent a good deal of time the night before brushing his hat until there wasn't a speck of dust left on it. He hoped Iris would notice all his effort. His face was shaved smooth as a riverbed stone and he had on a clean white shirt with a crisp celluloid collar that seemed only to be held in place by the black string tie that took him a great deal of time to tie to perfection. He hoped for a tense moment that he wasn't just wasting his time. After all Iris might already have a suitor who asked permission to escort her to the picnic. Maybe she never even gave Andrew a second thought after he left to go back east. He grimaced, shaking the baleful thought from his mind. If she felt about him any way near what he felt about her when they parted last summer, she would be there now waiting for him and hoping, as he was, that there was still a spark of love between them.

To make matters even worse, by the time he got back to the farm and had shoed Sparky his shirt was smudged with dirt and wet all the way down his back from sweat, and he smelled sour, like he'd been working in the hot sun all afternoon. His collar, that he had unfastened to make it easier to bend over, had popped open on one side while his string tie hung as lifeless as his bunch of wilted flowers. But once his mind was made up nothing was going to keep him from going to that picnic. He would just have to start all over and hope that he could recapture the look and feeling he had started the day off with.

CHAPTER NINE

While Iris was dressing for the picnic that morning she thought how proud her aunt would be. She swirled in front of the mirror. She looked the perfect picture of spring in her yellow sprigged muslin with the bow of pale green velvet tied perfectly at the small of her back, allowing the trailing ribbon to cascade over the fullness of her skirts. Iris actually felt pretty, looking the way she did with her hair swept up in French braids on either side of her face then tied at the nape of her neck where the remaining length fell down her back. She dabbed just a speck of liquid rouge, that Rebecca had given to her, on her lips then quickly pressed them together, hoping that Aunt Emma wouldn't notice. She smiled at the effect in the mirror. Sometimes wearing a dress could be a pleasant experience.

When she started down the stairs, her skirts swaying gaily along with her light steps. Through the windows on either side of the front door , she saw springboards and buggies approaching the house. "They're coming Aunt Emma!" she squealed over her shoulder just before she burst out onto the front porch looking like a daffodil in full bloom, waving to the people who waved back.

It didn't take long for the festivities to begin. Just as the first wagon load of visitors was arriving Edward joined Iris on the porch and together they greeted their guests. After Emma finished giving last minute instructions to Stella and Katie in the kitchen she appeared at the front door, wearing a garnet-colored broad cloth skirt and a smart looking white shirtwaist with a bouquet of simulated spring flowers pinned at her neck. With her hands clasped in front of her, her smile made it plain for all to see how pleased she was that they had come.

Before long there were scores of wagons and buggies lined up by the barn where Hickory was tending to the horses tethered in front of the water trough. Soon the whole yard was crowded with people. The women, with babies or toddlers, were sitting together on quilts near the shade, smiling at one another while they fed their little ones. The babies cried to be nursed while the older children chased each other in a game of tag. Already the girls starched bows were drooping and the boys knees were marked with grass stains and paw prints from several of the dogs who scampered beside them. The men, dressed in their Sunday suits and white shirts with taut suspenders, were standing around in small clusters, a few of them rolling cigarettes while they compared one another's progress with the spring planting. Iris walked around the yard, near the roses, where some little girls were giggling, sharing secrets. She passed the lilacs and finally sauntered over to the horses where she stayed for awhile petting their velvety muzzles. She listened to Dewey Woods, a bachelor who lived on a small farm a few miles down the road from them. His throaty laugh split the air and Iris knew that he was about to tell the little boys, hovering nearby, about the time when he lived in West Virginia and he was chopping wood when a copperhead snake bit him right on the tip of his forefinger. Faster than a blinding streak of lightening Dewey had flipped his hatchet and cut the snake in two. Then, without giving it a second thought, except to conclude that if he wasn't quick he would die, he used the same hatchet to whack off his finger. Iris didn't want to stay around to hear the rest of the gory story so she hurried off to look for Rebecca. When she finally spotted her, Rebecca was engrossed in a conversation with Todd Summers, a young man she had met at the county fair last summer.

As the day wore on Iris became downhearted. She grew tired of watching the men play horseshoes so she went back to the porch, hoping to catch a glimpse of Andrew, should he finally come riding up. It seemed she was destined to wait and wonder all by herself whether Andrew was going to come to the picnic or not. Where was a friend when you needed one? Maybe he was too busy working on the corral to come. She moved slowly along the deep porch, plucking at the lush green ferns engulfing the plant stands beside the pillars. She remembered to smile at the older women who were sitting in wicker chairs batting at flies while exchanging tidbits of news in their own little niches. She knew it was wrong to only pretend to be interested in what they were saying, but all she could think about was Andrew.

She offered to hold the Carlson's fussing baby so that Diane could feed her other two children, when in fact it gave Iris an excuse to continue to walk around while she kept a watchful eye on the road. Bouncing the baby in her arms she occasionally smiled, saying, 'yes' or 'no' or 'I'm not really sure' to questions that she paid little attention to. She was much too distracted by what she feared would turn out to be an embarrassing situation for her should Andrew fail to show up. Maybe this time she had let her imagination go too far, when in fact he didn't even care for her at all! Maybe Rebecca was right about Andrew. There was probably a girl back in Boston he cared for and Iris had simply been a passing fancy. She fought to disguise the worried look on her face. She wasn't ready to give up hope just yet. Still, when she looked toward the road there was a definite worrisome frown set between her brows.

The waiting and wondering was distressing enough but what rattled her most was Leo Branson having the nerve to show up all dressed up like a man who was going courting. With Andrew nowhere in sight all the effort she put into looking pretty for him only served to draw Leo's attention, perhaps confirming his insidious notion that she could be intimidated into changing her mind about marrying him.

Iris strolled back to Diane who had just finished fixing plates for her children and was sitting down again. Iris carefully laid the sleeping baby on a pallet near Diane's chair. Standing up straight she squared her shoulders. With her head tipped slightly back, she scanned the sky overhead.

"Looks like we might get some rain before nightfall," Diane said.

"I hope not. That'll ruin everything," Iris said as she continued gazing up at the sky. The once pleasant breeze had died down and the air was starting to feel close. Iris pulled a handkerchief out of her sleeve and waved it in front of her face while looking at Rebecca's Grandma Linnie who was snoozing with her chin resting on her chest.

"What's wrong, Iris?" Diane looked up at her.

Diane's voice seemed to Iris to be sailing off with a slow breeze up into the vanishing sky where the clanking sound of the game of horseshoes echoed. Looking slowly back at the sky, then at a canning jar on one of the side tables filled with pink roses entwined in ivy Iris numbly replied, "Oh, nothing. I'm a little sleepy that's all."

Diane looked at her watch that was pinned to the collar of her dress. "It's almost two o'clock. Maybe you ought to call the rest of the girls inside to rest before the dance tonight."

Iris dabbed her neck with her handkerchief. She didn't really feel the least bit tired; and besides it was too early to go inside to rest. Just when she concluded that maybe taking a nap would be about the most interesting thing that could happen the whole day, Mr. Schroeder, the head of the school board, mounted the porch steps and, with his hands held high, announced:

"Folks! Can I have your attention? It looks like we might get some rain, so if the young ladies will set their cakes out on the table behind me, we'll start the raffle a little early."

Every bit of mounted anticipation drained from Iris causing her to feel as weak and limp as the bow that once spanned her back like a beckoning flag. What was she going to do now? She stole one last look down the road and disappointment draped itself over her like a shroud. There was still no sign of Andrew.

CHAPTER TEN

When Mr. Schroeder announced that it was time for the raffle to begin, Iris' heart sank down to the soles of her shoes. Her throat constricted, followed by a hurtful swell inside of her chest. How could she have been so gullible? Andrew never wrote to her, he never promised that he would come back. All he did was kiss her goodbye. Yes, good-bye! What ever made her think that it was a kiss to seal a bond between them? She batted away the hot tears of disappointment that tipped her lashes as the crowd applauded when Amy Anderson's cake was won by Ryan Martin.

"Our next cake was baked by Rebecca Archer." Mr. Schroeder called out just as Rebecca came fluttering to Iris' side, bubbling over with excitement. "Who will be our first bidder?" his voice bellowed through the jostling crowd.

The crowd was beginning to gather in earnest just when Todd Summers shouted, "One dollar."

Rebecca contained a squeal but couldn't keep from bouncing up and down and clapping her hands. Iris' face broke out in an unexpected smile. She hoped Todd won the cake so that he and Rebecca could share it together. It would mean so much to Rebecca who was always busy helping her mother with the other children that she seldom had a chance to see Todd. Then Bill Sorenson raised one finger with a bid of, 'one twenty five' and Iris felt Rebecca wilt beside her.

"If he wins my cake I'm going home," Rebecca complained aloud.

"At least Todd's here to bid on your cake," Iris said before she even realized that she had said anything at all.

"Oh, Iris, I'm sorry." Rebecca turned to her friend with a consoling hand on Iris' shoulder just when Todd's voice rang out, 'One seventy five." A few of the girls standing along the porch railing squealed and a low mumble of voices filled the crowd as everyone waited for the next bid. When no one else spoke up Mr. Schroeder's baritone voice droned, "Miss Archer's banana cake goes to Mr. Todd Summers."

There was little time for reactions as Mr. Schroeder went on, picking up one cake after another until Iris thought she would go mad with anticipation. She grimaced at the look on Sara Fletcher's face when Bob Larson didn't win her cake. Iris thought that's what her face would look like if Andrew didn't show up and she had to go off with someone she didn't even want to look at. There was one more cake left then Mr. Schroeder would pick up hers. She raised her eyes, her neck stretching slightly as she tried to see down the length of Stoney Creek Road where there was a small cloud of dust stirring, but there was no sign of a horse and rider. Where was Andrew?

All at once, his voice resounding like a clanging dinner bell, Mr. Schroeder announced, "Our final cake was made by Miss Iris Stratton."

Iris felt Rebecca stiffen at her side just before Rebecca grabbed her hand that was clenched in the folds of her skirt. Holding her breath, Iris fought back the painful lump in her throat. She looked across the yard at Mr. Schroeder but could only see a blurred outline of his real self.

"Boy, it sure looks good," he said, stirring the crowd. "Who will be our first bidder?"

From the shuffling huddle of people a loud voice that Iris recognized as Tom Addy's called out, "Fifty cents."

Iris huffed, a scowl distorting her face. He was fourteen years old and his voice creaked like a rusty violin. After all the trouble that she went through! She would rather throw the cake at him, and his fifty cents too!

Another voice rang out, "Seventy-five cents," and Iris tried not to roll her eyes in disgust. Just about the time that Rebecca eagerly grabbed Iris' arm and began shaking it, Leo Branson presumptuously stepped forward and called out, "Two dollars."

A loud chorus of "ahhhs!" poured from the stirring crowd and the little girls standing in front of Mr. Schroeder started jumping up and down, clapping their hands and squealing gleefully as if they had just won the blessed prize.

Iris was furious! "How dare you! You despicable..." She clamped her mouth shut, feeling her face turning beet red as Rebecca's grip tightened on her arm. She didn't know anyone there who had enough money to bid higher than two dollars. Her heart began to race out of control, making it hard for her to catch her breath. She would gladly eat the cake with Tom Addy rather than come within a mile of Leo Branson.

"Oh, God," she pleaded under her breath. "Someone say, two fifty. I'll pay you back."

Mr. Schroeder threw his hand out toward the crowd. "Come on fellas, who can top two dollars?"

Bill Sorenson shouted from somewhere near the back of the crowd, 'Two seventy five." Someone in the huddle whistled shrilly and the ladies sighed in disbelief while Rebecca kept shaking Iris' arm and bouncing excitedly. Iris' face paled and she smiled wanly. She was ready to run out into the overwhelming huddle of men and grab Bill and kiss him right in front of everyone. But then she was shocked beyond comprehension when Leo's voice boomed above the steady hum of voices, "Four dollars!"

A gasp came from the ladies, like a sudden gust of March wind and the men shook their heads and groaned like the thunder that was just beginning to rumble in the distance. Iris heard someone say, 'If that don't beat all,' and her heart seemed to collapse inside of her. Mr. Schroeder's face beamed like a new father handing out cigars. He relished the competition, wanting it to continue.

"Sounds like we're in for a little bit of rain. You fella's better hurry up if you want to spend some time with the lady of your choice. Now who's going to bid higher than four dollars?"

Iris wanted to shout that he should be ashamed of himself. He was the head of the school board and here he was fanning contention. A minute passed, and then another. When no one offered a higher bid Mr. Schroeder prodded, his boisterous voice plainly building toward what would soon be his final gratitude speech. Rebecca stood still as a post beside Iris, her arms hanging at her sides; she was too stunned to speak. Iris was ready to turn around and run but instead she frantically searched the yard for her father. She finally caught sight of him standing at the end of the porch leaning against one of the pillars appearing calm, though looking somewhat pale as he kept a watchful eye on all that was going on. Did he still think that her marrying Leo Branson was a good idea? She squared her shoulders defiantly. This was her last chance to make it clear to everyone there that she would never marry Leo Branson. Mustering up the courage, she was ready to lunge forward but before she had the chance to voice her objections Emma appeared at her side, gripping her arm to hold her back, while placing a comforting hand around Iris' waist. She moved close to Iris, whispering near her ear.

"Don't worry; I had a little talk with your father today. He won't allow Leo Branson anywhere near you."

The words should have been a comfort to Iris but she was all too aware of the rules regarding the raffle. She caught her breath when Mr. Schroeder's hand went up, ready to finalize the bid. She looked eagerly toward the dimming sky just beyond the treetops, praying desperately for a sudden downpour. But, knowing that was wishful thinking and that her father wouldn't be allowed to bid on her cake, she refuted, "But how? What can he do now?"

Emma's eyes shifted protectively from Mr. Schroeder, who was still talking, over to Leo, and then back to Mr. Schroeder who was just about to lower his hand on Leo's bid. "Your father will let Leo pay the four dollars. Then he'll see to it that his money is refunded and that he's escorted off of our property."

Iris held her breath. There would be angry words, and possibly a fight. She couldn't allow that. What if her father got hurt? She would just have to grit her teeth and go off to the place of Leo's choice and eat her 'special' cake with him. She shuddered.

What a dreadful thought. But what other choice did she have?

"If there won't be another bidder willing to go higher than four dollars for Miss Stratton's scrumptious cake then the final bid goes to..."

"Ten dollars!"

A strong, unfamiliar voice carried over the top of the crowd cutting off Mr. Schroeder's closing words as the sound of clattering horse's hooves rent the air. For a minute there was dead silence as everyone turned in unison to gawk at the stranger. But the man wasn't a stranger to Iris who wanted to laugh and cry all in the same gulping breath. Everyone remained as still as a cat stalking a bird, watching, with eyes and mouths gaping wide. A tall angular man wearing a brown Stetson and a string tie swung out of his silver studded saddle and, with a quick slap on the flanks, sent his horse trotting off before he swept open his vest of midnight blue and withdrew a chiseled leather wallet. He slipped out a crisp ten dollar bill, deposited the wallet, and then with his arms creating a path through the awestruck crowd he strode with the confidence of a banker up to Mr. Schroeder who dumbfounded accepted the bill in exchange for the lopsided chocolate cake.

The spell was broken when someone in the crowd yelled, "Yehaw!" and everyone started clapping wildly. There was a clamor of talking then another shrill whistle before Dewey whipped out his harmonica and started playing a frolicking tune. The crowd dispersed, murmuring like the thunder overhead while each bidder headed for the lady of his choice. When all the raucous died down the mothers were dabbing their eyes and rocking their babies busily, and the little girls were no longer jumping up and down but had suddenly turned as shy as pansies exposed to the afternoon sun. The older women stayed on the porch away from the breeze the storm was pushing in. With mouths pursed they were too awestruck to speak. Instead, with their heads to one side, their faces hidden in their bonnets they kept their eyes meekly turned away from the handsome stranger. In a moments time their knitting needles were clicking faster than Dewey could play the spoons on his bent knee. The young men were talking loud and boisterously, commenting with a jerk of their fist on how close Leo Branson, who seemed to have disappeared after the final bid, came to stealing a kiss from Stratton's daughter. The older men simply shook their heads, saying they'd never seen the like...a man bidding ten whole dollars on a cake. He must be plumb loco. By then Dewey Woods was leaning against a tree, playing a soft tune, Iris imagining him filing the events of this day away for a time when he could tell a group of gangly boys how one hot afternoon a tall, handsome stranger came riding across the windblown prairie with his heart in his vest pocket, and how he won all the ladies' hearts, not to mention the respect of every boy and man in the county, though they'd never admit it in a coon's age.

Rebecca, who was still standing beside Iris was crying unabashedly, tears flickering down her face, her lips pressed tightly together while Emma, who was too choked up to speak clung to her niece's trembling shoulders. Iris' hands were pressed tightly against her flaming cheeks, her fingertips covering her mouth that was quivering with the urge to cry out Andrew's name. As he walked toward her, his arresting eyes fixed on hers, she looked at him through a cloud of happy tears. She knew full well that her heart was rushing blindly toward an untold journey, an emotional ride was welling up inside of her unlike any she had ever seen, even at horse breaking time.

Andrew, as chivalrous as any knight, mounted the steps. He crossed the porch, his boots firmly striking the floor boards, a sound that told everyone he was there to stay. When he stopped a few feet from Iris and smiled proudly, Iris looked meekly at her father whose soft smile gave her the permission she longed for. Her aunt kissed her briefly on the cheek and Iris swiftly picked up her picnic hamper before placing her trembling fingers in Andrew's beckoning hand.

They walked away together, Andrew leading Iris to the spot just beneath the tree where last summer he sat at her feet and together they dreamed of such a time as this. When he got up to leave that day so long ago, he had left his heart behind and now he was back to claim it.

When they got to the tree he turned around and smiled at her. She smiled back and the world and everything in it seemed to stand still. The only sound in the entire universe was the sound of his heart hammering against his chest. He could forget dreaming about the coming of pounding horse flesh. There was a stampede of his own making going on inside of him, causing a fiery path to course through his veins and it was aimed straight at his heart, the vibrations channeling through his body like a thundering herd of wild mustangs. It took every bit of willpower he could muster to hold back the mounting desire to sweep Iris into his arms and kiss her right there in front of God and everyone. For now he would have to be content to sit beside her on the wisps of new grass beneath the shade tree and hope that she could read in his eyes what he was unable to say with his lips.

Iris set the hamper down, then lifted the lid and pulled out a large blue and white checkered cloth which she whipped out in front of her then watched as it floated into place among the flickering shadows on the ground around them.

Andrew waited for her to sit down before he sat across from her, setting the cake between them. If only there weren't so many curious eyes boring in their direction. Then he could sit beside her with his shoulder touching hers. There were so many things that he wanted to say, starting with why he never wrote.

Their eyes met briefly and Iris quickly turned her head away. After all the months she'd been planning what to say if she ever saw Andrew again, and now she couldn't remember one word that she'd written down. She reached into the straw hamper pulling out two small china plates, a set of silver forks and the white napkins that she had packed so carefully the night before. She wasn't sure if she looked away to conceal the question in her eyes or to display the expected lady-like behavior in the presence of so many gawking eyes. She hadn't anticipated feeling uncomfortable in this situation. She chanced a quick side-long glance in Andrew's direction. Why couldn't she just look him straight in the eye and ask him why he never wrote? The thought no sooner left her than the answer sprang from her heart. If she looked into Andrew's big brown eyes now the color of burnished amber with the sunlight flickering off his lashes, her insides would absolutely melt. To hide the blush on her cheeks she turned her shoulder, holding her face sideways as she reached inside the basket for a cake knife and began cutting a wedge from the cake. When she pulled back the knife, she frowned unexpectedly.

"What's the matter?" Andrew looked worried. Maybe she had planned to eat the cake with someone else.

Iris shook her head rapidly. "Nothing."

Then why did she feel the sudden urge to cry? Something didn't look right. There was a big gaping hole in the middle of her cake and it was full of icing. When she looked up to see if Andrew had noticed it there was a perplexed look on his face. "Is this piece big enough?" She fought the tears in her voice.

Andrew wondered what happened to the cake but decided this didn't seem to be the time to ask. Instead he nodded as quick and eager as he could, his hand outstretched to receive his prize. He shoved a fork full of sugary icing into his mouth while reminding himself how much he liked eating the icing and leaving the cake when he was a boy.

"This sure is good," he said with as much enthusiasm as he could bolster. It was worth all of his exaggerating just to see the way Iris' face lit up when he took another bite.

For a soft lingering moment neither one said a word, though Andrew's eyes took in the radiance of Iris' flouncing yellow skirt that half covered his leg and Iris peeked beneath her fanning lashes at a shock of Andrew's chestnut brown hair that teased his right eyebrow, making him look like a feisty schoolboy. When the silence grew heavy between them, they both spoke at once, their words colliding. They burst into embarrassed laughter.

"Go ahead," Andrew said as he set his plate down beside the toppled cake. He leaned back against the tree and was instantly filled with longing when Iris looked at him with her large, doe-shaped eyes.

A cluster of sparrows were flittering in and out of the bushes beside the road while the sound of children playing a game of blind man's bluff carried through the air. Iris noticed that Andrew had a few grey smudges on his shirt and that his collar was on crooked. Andrew was wondering when would be the right time to touch her hand laying flat on the cloth beside her without appearing brash.

"I...I heard that you're building a corral over at the Stevens' place," Iris remarked.

"Word sure gets around," Andrew said.

"That's how it is out here. I hope you don't mind that we all knew you were coming."

Andrew shook his head. "No. Not at all. That's what I like about being here, everyone's so friendly. They all seem to look out for one another."

Iris paused, wondering if she should thank him for rescuing her from Leo Branson. "Thank you for bidding on my cake. I...I hope you liked it."

Andrew was quick to nod his head. "Sure. I mean it was great." His lips formed a line. "I picked some flowers for you but they died. I guess it was too hot."

Iris blushed, shrugging her shoulders lightly. "That's all right." She wondered if she should offer him another piece of cake, but decided against it when she looked up and saw her father lighting the lanterns near the platform.

"Everyone's been talking about the horses coming in." Iris hoped her words didn't sound too practiced.

"I can hardly wait to head out to meet them," Andrew answered. He knew he should say something else but what could he say without sounding too forward?

They sat quietly thinking to themselves when Iris lifted her eyes to meet his. For a moment every sound around them dulled and any movement simply disappeared.

Debra L. Hall

"If Aunt Emma will let me, I'm going to watch the horses come in from on top of the ridge," Iris said, breaking the spell.

"I'd like that." Andrew reached out and touched Iris' hand. "Knowing that you'll be out there watching me will make the ride all the more exciting."

Smiling, Iris turned her head and saw Hickory sprinkling cornmeal on the dance floor. The men who would be playing for the dance were starting to get into position. It was too late for Aunt Emma to suggest the girls go in for a nap. Iris was ready to dance.

"It looks like they're getting ready for the dance," Iris said, hoping the rain would hold off for awhile in case Andrew should ask her to dance. Even if it did rain she wouldn't mind, her heart was doing all of her dancing for her.

CHAPTER ELEVEN

The waning sun had slipped in and out of the gathering clouds all afternoon and was now hanging wearily in the western sky. A soft wind that smelled of the coming rain was beginning to stir the treetops while the sound of thunder rumbling across the plains made everyone eager to start the dance. The varying sounds of tuning instruments plucked the air, creating a festive mood. After settling the children down for their naps the mothers went outside where everyone was headed for the dance platform. Iris took her hamper into the kitchen then hurried to the porch, having firmly fixed in mind dancing with Andrew for most of the evening. But, when she looked over at the tree where she left him, he was leaning against the tree trunk with his broad shoulders held back and his thumbs hooked inside his vest pockets. He was surrounded by so many flirting girls that their billowing skirts formed a colorful bouquet. How could he stand there looking so interested in front of all those girls after the trouble she went through to make a cake for him? Confused and hurt, Iris whirled around ready to storm back into the house when she ran head long into Kemp Spencer, who stumbled over his words in an attempt to ask her for the first dance. She could hardly refuse him, seeing the way his eyes lit up when she smiled weakly at him. She followed him across the yard to the dance platform forcing herself to keep her head raised and a pleasant smile on her face. Iris stepped onto the platform, placing her unwilling hand into Kemp's wide, rough palm. When he put his arm around her waist she tried not to wince. Forgetting about all the dancing that had gone on in her heart only a short time ago, she concluded that she would have fun even if Andrew never asked her to dance.

...

Andrew turned his head away from the flock of inquisitive eyes and saw Iris whirling on the dance floor with a tall willowy boy who couldn't be more than eighteen. She had a smile on her face and her head was held higher than a strutting peacock. With his shoulders thrown back and his hand clamped on Iris' waist the boy was trying his darnedest to impress her.

Andrew cast a baleful eye over the many dancing couples. Seeing how many eager young men there were, all of them spiffed up and ready to dance with any girl who was willing, he wondered what ever made him think that Iris was just waiting for him to ask her to dance.

Just then Iris, in the arms of that red faced boy whose smile was wider than a half moon, whirled near the outer edge of the floor in plain view of Andrew. What was he so happy about? Andrew huffed silently. Iris was probably mad at him after all that time of not writing and then he waltzes in here bidding a gambler's winnings for her cake without even thinking about asking her to dance. If she only knew how wrung out his heart was she would understand his reason for forgetting. He never could figure out women and their sensitivities. She could've told him she wanted to dance with him. Well, if she was happy in the arms of that wisp of a man then let her dance with him all night. The couple flew by again and Andrew's neck craned. He could dance better than that. Just then a grumbling thunder rolled overhead. He wasn't there to be a judge in a dance contest. If he was going to do any dancing tonight he'd better hurry before it started to rain. He stepped forward and picking out one of the girls standing closest to him he led her to the dance floor.

One dance led to another, Iris being pulled further away from Andrew first by one stiff-legged farmer, then by a fumbling hired hand before she was all but tossed back into the arms of Kemp, who didn't seem to want to dance with anyone but her. She couldn't help but notice that Andrew had danced several dances with Judy Webber. Of all the girls there he would pick her. Iris would never hear the end of how Andrew bid on her cake but then danced all night with Judy Webber. She scowled when she saw them laughing as Andrew twirled Judy around with her arm in the air. Iris wondered where he learned to dance like that. No doubt some debutant back in Boston showed him all the right steps.

When the song ended Iris thought about dancing with her father but her aunt told her that he wasn't feeling well and had gone inside to rest. There wasn't even a moment's time to ask what was the matter with him before Iris was approached by one of Rebecca's brothers. As much as she hated to she had to decline, promising to dance with him as soon as she was rested. Making her way through the milling couples she passed Rebecca and Todd, who didn't even seem to notice her. She stepped off the platform and leaning against one of the lantern posts, she fanned herself with her handkerchief.

Iris knew it wasn't right but she couldn't help feeling a twinge of jealousy every time she saw Rebecca whirling across the floor in Todd's arms, looking so pretty in the red and blue plaid dress that she had hemmed for her. When she happened to catch another glimpse of Andrew, he was spinning some other hopeful girl around the dance floor. Iris would just have to accept the fact that he was going to ignore her the rest of the night. Hot tears stung her lashes and she quickly brushed them away. She couldn't blame him. He was probably angry at her for having spent more than a week's wages on her cake that was nothing but a few crumbs and a blob of icing. Maybe it would help if she got the money back from Mr. Schroeder.

The twilight sky mingled with the dove gray clouds moving swiftly overhead. A couple of men were hitching up their wagons preparing to leave and some of the women were beginning to pack their hampers after folding up their quilts. The song ended and Andrew walked across the yard to where he'd left his hat under the tree. He stood there alone for a lingering moment, wondering if he would ever get the chance to talk to Iris again. It seemed she was having a good time dancing with everyone who asked her. He lowered his head, fitting on his Stetson. He didn't have anyone to blame but himself. He should have taken the chance that Edward Stratton would discover his letters and written to her anyway. At least she would've known that he loved her and wanted to be with her more than anyone else in all the world. Then she would be dancing in his arms and not those of some other man's.

...

Iris listened to the sound of the windmill vanes turning as she watched Hickory walk toward the silhouetted barn with a galvanized pail in his hand. He was going to milk the cows. She wished she could go with him. She'd rather be anywhere else than dancing with every available man in the county, most of them it seemed wanting to dance with her at the same time, all except for Andrew.

One song ended and everyone clapped just before another one was about to begin. Before Iris even had a chance to catch her breath Rebecca's brother was back asking her to dance again. It would be rude to fabricate another reason why she couldn't accept so she gave him her hand. Just before he swung her onto the dance floor she cast a furtive glance along the side lines where she was surprised to see Andrew standing all alone, his face partially hidden beneath the brim of his Stetson. She wondered if he was getting ready to leave. Before she knew it she was being tossed every which way, while somehow managing to keep at least one foot on the floor. She caught another glimpse of Andrew tipping his hat to Judy just as the music was ending and no matter how hard she tried she couldn't hold back the tears. A few large plops of rain fell and Iris wiped her face, hoping Ted hadn't noticed that she was crying. Slowly everyone began to leave the platform, the women hurrying toward the house to get the children and the men heading to the barn to hitch up their horses. Just when Iris thought about leaving she noticed that her skirt was hooked on something. She tugged on it gently but it was held fast. She told Ted to go on before he got wet then she bent over to unsnag her skirt.

Suddenly a bulking figure loomed up from under the platform and white glaring eyes shot from a face smeared black with charcoal. A deep throaty voice growled, "I told you I'd be back," so near to her ear that Iris could almost feel the bristles on the intruder's face. She let out a shattering scream that pierced through the sound of the low rumbling thunder. There was a crack of lightening followed by an onslaught of rain. People started running in all directions, their shoes hammering on the wooden platform. She let out another scream while jerking frantically at her skirt, but the fiend held her fast, at last succeeding in pulling her off the dance floor and onto the ground at his feet. Then all at once he vanished and, looking up, she saw Andrew vault over the rail around the platform and chase after him.

Iris shouted, "Andrew stop!"

A man's voice rose above the storm, "Everything's all right. Everyone hurry and get out of the rain."

One of the men helped Iris to her feet and before she knew it she was running into the dark after Andrew who was on the ground wrestling with the man who had pulled her off the dance floor. There was a loud thud and a muffled groan before Iris saw Andrew fall over and the hulking figure run off into the darkness. Andrew lunged forward but Iris grabbed his arm.

"Stop! It's Leo. He'll kill you. No! Andrew. Don't go after him."

They fell into each others arms, breathless, Iris crying while Andrew covered her face with the warmth of his fumbling hands. "Iris, oh, Iris are you all right? Did he hurt you?"

Still shaking and unable to speak clearly, Iris shook her head, her reply sounding like a baby blubbering.

Some men came running across the yard just as Andrew was drawing Iris to her feet.

"Is she all right?"

Iris recognized Hickory's voice. "Yes." She caught her breath. "Yes. I'm coming."

"Iris! Iris, where are you?"

Iris looked up and saw her father running across the yard carrying a bobbing lantern in his hand.

"Iris, are you all right?" With one arm Edward pulled her to his side where she dropped her head against his wet trembling shoulder. With calm words Iris sought to comfort him as he led her toward the house.

Iris stopped to look behind her. She placed a reassuring hand on her father's arm, her eyes filled with tenderness. "Father, I need to talk to Andrew. Please don't worry. Leo's gone and Andrew will be here. I'll be all right."

As Andrew approached Edward motioned for Hickory to leave. Then looking Andrew straight in the eye he spoke in an even tone. "I'll be waiting up for her. Stay on the porch and see to it that she gets safely inside before you leave."

Andrew nodded. "Yes sir."

Edward led his daughter to the porch then went inside and brought out a shawl for her. He mounted the lantern on a nail to the left of the door then without another word he left Andrew and Iris standing alone on the porch.

CHAPTER TWELVE

As with love, so tender is the prairie

Draping her aunt's shawl around her shoulders, Iris sat on one of the wicker chairs near the front steps. With her wet hair clinging to her face and her drooping yellow dress splattered with mud she looked like a drenched pansy. She listened to the soft rain falling just beyond the porch wondering if she should apologize for the cake.

Andrew sat on one of the chairs next to her, carefully studying her face for any sign of pain. "Are you all right, Iris? He didn't hurt you did he?"

Iris nervously shook her head. "No. I mean yes." Her shoulders dropped with a weak laugh. "No, he didn't hurt me and yes, I'm all right, except for being drenched."

Relieved, Andrew sat back with his head bent, his fingers sliding around the brim of his hat in his lap. He ran his spread fingers through his wet hair in an effort to keep it off his forehead, wishing he could think of some way to apologize for not asking Iris to dance with him. With the party over and the music gone he figured he'd be better off if he avoided the subject altogether. At last he broke the silence, his voice somewhat hesitant, betraying him the way it always did when he was in a fix.

"Did you read the book of poems I left with you last summer?" He felt like a gangling school boy stumbling over his big feet.

"Yes, I did," Iris replied, trying with all her might to appear prim and lady-like, the way her aunt had taught her. She smiled softly at his awkwardness. "Did you miss your glove?" She asked coyly.

"My glove!" Andrew's head shot up. "You had it all this time."

"You left it on the grass, and you can't have it back."

"Humph," Andrew rallied, turning his head as if studying

79

the darkness beyond the porch steps. "Instead of having a cattle rustler on my hands I'm faced with a wily woman who it appears has something cunning up her sleeve."

"Nooo!" Iris dragged out her denial. "It's just mine now, that's all."

"And what do I get in return?" Andrew refused to give up.

"Cold hands!" Iris giggled then remembered herself and immediately covered her mouth with a clasped hand.

Andrew was silent, imagining her blushed cheeks behind her slender fingers.

Iris wondered if her aunt would say that she had overstepped the bounds of propriety by speaking out of line.

Thinking back on the night's events they both spoke at once, "I'm sorry," then stopped abruptly, their heads turned, their eyes discreetly falling to one side.

"Iris." Andrew bent forward, his deep voice spoke softly. "I...I wanted to dance with you but when I saw you out there dancing with all those ..."

"Oh, Andrew," Iris' head shot up. "They mean nothing to me. I just...well, when they asked me I just couldn't say no."

"I thought it was because I never wrote."

Iris' eyes widened. "I thought it was because of the cake."

Andrew frowned. "The cake?"

"It wasn't worth a whole ten dollars. I'll try to get your money back."

A laugh escaped Andrew and he fell on his knees at Iris' feet. With his hands gripping the arms of her chair his eyes implored her. "Iris." He looked at her wet hair. "My sweet little drooping flower. I don't want my money back. Just being here with you made it worth every penny."

Iris dropped her gaze, her hands folded in her lap. "You mean you would've rather danced with me than Judy Webber?"

Andrew reached out and laid his hand against the side of

Iris' neck where he brushed clinging strands of black hair away from her cheek with his thumb. Her skin was just the way he remembered it, causing his heart to rush with desire. "Judy was a girl that I whirled across a dance floor but you were the girl that whirled across my heart."

Despite the cool breeze whispering across the porch, Iris blushed warmly as Andrew continued smoothing her cheek. "I didn't think I'd ever see you again," she whispered guilelessly, on the verge of tears.

"I wanted to write, to tell you that I would be back someday. Please believe that. There were so many things I wanted to say but...I knew that your father disapproved, and there was no other way to get a letter to you."

Tears splashed down Iris' face. "I thought you came back because of the horses."

"That was my excuse. But I couldn't stay away any longer. Horses or not I couldn't keep my mind off of you." Andrew cradled her face in his hands that smelled of wind and rain. "Iris, I'm sorry I made you cry."

Iris shook her head, a tremulous laugh escaping between her sobs. "You didn't make me cry. I...I'm just so happy that you're finally here."

Iris' heart quickened and she threw her arms around Andrew's neck, her tears sprouting warm on his firm jaw. Andrew, no longer able or willing to hold back the desire came to his feet, and pulling Iris up beside him he drew her away from the door, where Edward waited on the other side, before he pulled her tightly into his arms and kissed her. Their hearts collided; their whispers were full of unuttered poetry that blended with the melody of the rain trickling from the down spouts.

His hands spanned her back and the feel of her in his arms was electrifying, the reality of all his past imaginings. "I love you," he confessed in the warm hollow of her ear.

Iris drew back and Andrew waited for her to speak but she remained silent, hesitant at first, fighting the lump that surged up from her heart and was now lodged in her throat. Andrew was gone for so long that she had almost forgotten what he looked like. With her hand fanned against his chest she studied his sizable frame, the span of his shoulders, the reckless curls that left their assigned place and were again tumbling over his forehead near his beckoning eyes. She hadn't realized until now how desperately she had missed him. The beginning of a smile drew her back into his arms. "Don't ever leave me again," she begged.

Holding her close, Andrew clutched Iris' hands in his and showered her fingertips with kisses. When he spoke there was quiet resolve in his voice. "A herd of wild horses couldn't drag me away. A will stronger than fate drew me to these plains, and now I'm here to stay."

Iris laughed, and then suddenly without regard for all that she had been taught was proper she showered Andrew's face with kisses. "Oh Andrew," she laughed tremblingly, "I know why I love you now. You're a poet and your heart is full of unfinished poetry. I want to be your song and the rhythm that moves you."

"Then that's the way it'll be." Andrew studied her face. "I don't know why I stayed away so long," he said. "I've been tortured by the memory of you, never knowing if you felt the same way about me."

There was no need of a reply. The lamplight reached out and engulfed them, two as one, their touching faces turned toward the sound of the abating rain just beyond the spindled porch rail. Iris sighed, not realizing she had until Andrew's head turned next to her face. She felt herself blush, hoping beyond hope that he didn't think she sighed because she was tired of his presence. Her very being never felt so full of warm feelings and escalating emotions, all of them gathering near her heart where they were weaving memories.

Andrew smiled softly to himself, pleased at how good a sigh could feel. A moment lingered on, then Andrew reached for his hat whipping back his unruly hair before positioning it. He led Iris to the door and they stood apart, each absorbing the aftermath of confessed love when Andrew looked out into the still, dark night.

"I have to ride into town tomorrow to pick up Mr. Stevens' cousin. She's coming in from St. Louis. I'd like to see you tomorrow night if it's all right with you."

Iris gently touched his face before she kissed him. "Only if you'll stay longer next time."

"You got yourself a deal," Andrew said pulling her closer.

Iris laid her head against his chest, cherishing the sound of his heartbeat so close to hers.

"I'll be riding out to meet John with the horses day after tomorrow."

"I hope you..."

Suddenly a rifle shot sounded, Andrew's hat flew off his head and Iris' scream pierced the air. Andrew whipped around and grabbed her, pulling her into the shadows away from the lamplight just as the targeted bullet glanced off the door frame. Fleeting horse's hooves rent through the night sky and the door flew open shattering the beveled glass against the side of the house. Edward came hurling through the entry cocking his rifle as he charged down the steps yelling toward the bunk house for Hickory to saddle up his horse. Iris cried out and Edward shouted, "Get her out of here!" Fear pumped wildly through Iris, firing her determination to flee but Andrew's strong, sure hands gripped her upper arms from behind and he pulled her flailing body back, her toes barely touching the floor. Andrew whirled Iris around, pulling her to face him before she finally quit struggling and fell with a limp cry in his arms.

The quiet around them suddenly filled with the sound of heels snapping in the entry followed by Emma's frantic appeal. Andrew shouted, "Get away from the door!" There was a gasp and the sound of a quick retreat just before Edward stomped back up the steps shouting orders at Hickory who was following close at his heels hauling his wide suspenders over his union suit.

"Saddle up my horse. If that shyster thinks he's going to get away with this he's got another guess coming."

Hickory ran off toward the barn while Edward stormed into the house and Andrew followed him with one of Iris' wrists held captive in his firm grip. When Emma heard them coming she ran toward Iris who was clinging to Andrew's side. Letting go of Iris, Andrew immediately turned to Edward.

"I'm going with you."

"Andrew, no!" Iris cried.

Andrew's eyes remained fixed on Edward.

"Go home Burgess, this has nothing to do with you," Edward ordered.

Andrew stood his ground, his eyes radiating cold refusal. "When someone takes a pot shot at my head I'd say it has plenty to do with me."

Edward pried open his rifle and peered inside. "I can settle this on my own."

"I'm sure you can, but since Branson came calling on me this time I'm going to answer his call and be done with it. You can come along if you like but he's mine for the taking." Without waiting for a reply Andrew turned and strode with purpose out of the house.

A short while later both men sat mounted in front of the house. Emma and Iris were standing on the porch and Hickory was standing on the bottom step with a loaded rifle cradled in his right arm.

"You two stay inside," Edward commanded and Emma began pulling Iris toward the shattered front door. "Hickory, I want you to board up that window, and then stay on the porch until we get back."

"I wish you wouldn't go," Iris addressed her father, her eyes clinging to Andrew.

Emma leveled a sharp eye on Edward. "Can't this wait until morning, Edward? It's dark and it could be dangerous."

"No telling where he'll be by daylight," Edward

answered. Seizing the leather reins he nudged his horse around to face the road.

Once again the night was quiet, except for the faint chinking of bridles just before Edward and Andrew rode off into the darkness.

CHAPTER THIRTEEN

Through the patchy moonlight and the rain that blew from the eerie shadows cast by the trees along side the road, the two horsemen galloped toward an uncertain destiny. The damp wind braced Andrew's face smelling strongly of wet earth and pulsing horse flesh. Who would have thought that only yesterday he was putting up a corral for a herd of wild horses and now, a day later, he was chasing after a man who had tried to kill him over a woman.

Andrew looked at Edward Stratton and could feel the tension that remained between them. He wondered why Stratton let him sit on the porch with his daughter when he once swore to shoot him if he even set foot on Stratton land. Now they were riding out together after a man who proved more of a threat to Stratton than Andrew had ever been.

Andrew drew back his reins as Edward slowed his horse who twitched against the bridle, eager to continue the chase. Edward scanned the road just ahead and the trees that gently shook the rain from their branches.

"You hear anything?" Edward turned his head toward Andrew while keeping a guarded eye on the road ahead.

"Just the wind," Andrew replied.

Edward was quiet for a long time, slowly nudging his horse ahead. Andrew kept his horse a few paces behind Edward, watching and waiting for any sign of danger. The stillness was interrupted by the sound of the horses' hooves clopping rhythmically on the gravel road and by the raindrops plopping onto their hats from the outstretched boughs overhead. The road forked and to the left the dark shape of a house appeared in a small clearing. When Edward pulled up the slack on his reins he turned and motioned to Andrew, who then slipped down into the ditch before disappearing into the trees. Edward leveled his rifle just above the horse's head.

"Branson! Get yourself out here," he shouted toward the

house.

There was no reply. Edward watched guardedly for any sign of movement, waiting for a light to appear in one of the windows. When nothing happened he cocked his rifle and blasted the sky above his head.

"I'll start putting out the windows next," his baritone voice echoed through the still yard.

A minute dragged by when, from inside the house, there was a noise like that of a heavy table scraping across a wooden floor. The door opened cautiously and a lanky stooped man shouldered his way through the entry.

"Don't shoot," a scraggly voice groveled as the man stepped onto the porch grappling a twisted pair of suspenders over his shoulders.

"Step off the porch, slow and easy," Edward spoke sharply, moving the rifle barrel to indicate where he wanted the man to stand.

"Who says I have ta?" The silhouetted figure hauled back his shoulders.

In one swift move Andrew leaped deftly over the porch rail and had the man's arm twisted behind his back before he could turn around, the barrel of Andrew's pistol brandished under the man's hooked nose.

"This says you have to," Andrew directed the man's steps off the porch and a few feet into the yard.

Edward walked his horse closer so he could get a better look at the man. He didn't recognize who he was, nor did he care. "I don't have any qualms to settle with you. I'm here to see Branson."

The man jerked Andrew off his shoulder, letting out a derisive snort. "Well, he ain't here."

Edward groaned then pulled the trigger and a bullet tore up the muddy ground at the stranger's feet. The man let out a disconcerted cry and flew backward against Andrew's stalwart frame.

"I ain't lyin' mister. Branson's gone. He left me to look after the place till they get back."

"When did he leave?" Andrew quizzed tersely, his hat brim touching the man's gristled face.

"B'out an hour ago."

"I got another bullet here says you know where they're headed," Edward said, raising the rifle barrel.

"I don't see where that's any of your business mister. He's gone; that's all you gotta..."

A bullet clipped the man's ragged sleeve. He yelped and went sprawling to the ground with Andrew scrambling next to him, his gun teetering in his hand.

"Hold your fire," Andrew cried out. "He's not going anywhere."

"Well, I don't have all night. Either he tells us where Branson's at or I cut a notch in his other sleeve to match."

The man sprawled in the mud, struggling to his feet with his livid eyes fixed on Edward. "Him and that boy o' his are headed for Boston. All they said was they got business to tend to. They never said when they was comin' back."

"Boston," Edward repeated, a hint of breathless apprehension in his voice. "Let him go." He motioned for Andrew to mount up. "Let's get out of here."

Andrew frowned. "You aren't buying that story are you?"

"I swear, it's the truth," the man defended. "Branson said he was goin' to Boston to look for some woman. As if there ain't enough of em' around here."

"I said, let's go!" Edward shouted. "That shyster won't get away with this."

Andrew dropped his hold on the man and watched him stumble backwards, ready for him should he pull a pistol out of his waistband. The man leered back at Andrew, swearing under his breath as he turned and shuffled back up onto the porch. The door slammed shut before Andrew returned his gun to his waistband

and began slapping the mud from his pants.

"What was that all about?" he asked, walking toward his horse without looking up at Stratton who seemed suddenly to have lost his gumption.

"Branson's gone. Take my word for it." Edward lashed back before he whipped his horse around and flew off into a gallop.

Andrew swept up his reins then swung into his saddle shouting, "Giddap", while pulling his horse into a half turn as they lunged toward the road.

With the damp wind in his face he rode hard and fast to catch up with Stratton who was half way down the road by the time Andrew caught sight of him. He was riding like a mad man, whipping his horse frantically with the length of his reins. What had suddenly gotten into him? Andrew thought he should be glad to hear that the Bransons were gone, but instead he was riding hell bent like there was no tomorrow.

Hickory, who it appeared had been dozing on the porch step, clattered to his feet when Edward came charging into the yard. Ignoring the startled guard, Edward abruptly reined in, hurled from the saddle and took the steps two at a time. Andrew rode into the yard in time to see him stop outside the door where he braced himself against the door frame and propped his head on his outstretched arm. Andrew flew out of the saddle and leaped up the porch steps before Edward calmly turned around to face him. "You'd better leave, Burgess."

Andrew's first inclination was to question Stratton about what went wrong, but he could tell by Edward's stern look and the tight set of his jaw that he wasn't about to tolerate any questions. Just then the front door swung open and Emma appeared with a lighted lamp in her hand. Iris was standing inquiringly at her side. Against the yellow lamplight Andrew couldn't see the expression on Iris' face but he was sure by her stance that it was one of concern.

"Go inside. I'll be in in a minute," Edward's eyes met the

lamplight.

Andrew wanted to say good night, and to tell Iris that Branson was gone, but he figured his best bet was to remount and ride out as fast as he could. Whatever it was that was bothering Stratton it was none of his business.

...

Gathering his composure, Edward watched Andrew ride away before he spoke to Hickory. "Wait here. I have a letter that needs to be delivered tonight to my solicitor, Richard Harwick."

Hickory nodded while fumbling with his hat. "You okay, Mr. Stratton?"

"I'll be fine," Edward coarsely replied.

"I'll go saddle up my horse," Hickory said as he turned and walked away. He was halfway across the yard and hidden by the darkness before Edward gathered a shaky breath and turned to go inside.

He shut the door behind him hoping that Emma and Iris would think he was just tired from the day's activities. He remained unaware of the blatant ire that reddened his face and set up the veins in his neck.

Watching, as Edward struggled to control the fact that he was disturbed, Emma discreetly waited for him to speak while Iris rushed to his side placing her hand protectively on his arm.

"Father, what happened? What's the matter?"

Edward tossed his hat aside and began to climb out of his jacket. "They weren't there," he answered, handing his coat to Emma. Quickly he turned to go into his study, concealing the disconcerted look on his face. "Emma, get me some paper and something to write with. If Branson wants to play this cat and mouse game he can play it with my solicitor." With his hand hovering on the porcelain door knob Edward turned briefly. "Iris, it's time to go to bed."

"But father..."

"You've had a long day. Branson's gone, so there's nothing to be afraid of."

"Aren't you tired father?" Iris' voice softened.

Edward walked into the room disguising the uneasiness in his voice. "I'll be up shortly. Don't worry yourself, now."

The door shut softly and Emma placed a comforting hand on Iris' shoulders. "Your father's had a long day. He just needs a little time to himself. You need to get some rest now."

"Are you sure father's going to be all right?" Iris' eyes remained fixed on the closed door.

"Yes, dear. Now go to bed," Emma reassured.

...

Upstairs, Iris reluctantly crawled into the bed rubbing the chilling goose bumps along her arms and legs until she felt warm. All the while her thoughts vacillated between concern for her father, who appeared overly distraught, to warm tingly thoughts of Andrew. She found herself smiling for no apparent reason. A wild yearning was blossoming inside her breast, making her feel more beautiful than the morning sun whispering near the brim of the prairie, or the twilight sky as it softly brushed its violet hues over the countryside. All those months while Andrew was away he seemed only a figment of her imagination, a dream she had conjured up from the unwritten poetry deep inside her very being. But in his arms tonight there was no doubt that he was real. One moment the thought of loving Andrew, and no other man across the entire plains, was frightening and the next moment it was more exhilarating than a sudden spring shower. She saw him as he came galloping toward the crowd of bidders, his vest flying open, his hat propped back on his unruly head of hair. When his long stride reached out toward her, her heart was his. But it was his kiss that later claimed her, and now there was no turning back.

With the warm feeling of desire tucked safely away, Iris snuggled down into the fresh scent of wind blown sheets. Curling on her side with her eyes closed and her arms crossed tightly over her breasts, she could feel her heart beating rapidly. For a fleeting unforbidden moment she imagined Andrew's heart beating next to hers and she blushed in the dark.

She suddenly sat up, a perplexed look on her face. She didn't know that Jacob Stevens had a cousin from St. Louis. Iris wondered how long she was going to stay. And why did Andrew have to go in to town to get her? Iris gathered a disconcerted breath and plopped back down on her pillows. There was nothing to worry about. The woman was no doubt married, and if not, she was probably an old spinster.

CHAPTER FOURTEEN

Andrew lay in his bed in the dark, unable to erase the image of Iris standing beside her Aunt in the open doorway with the light filtering through her streaming ebony hair. The thought triggered feelings of longing that he had no right to claim. Iris Stratton was worth more than a ten dollar cake and he knew it. She was a sensitive, spontaneous woman whose emotions he knew could not be trifled with. He had no intention of leading her on. When the time was right he was going to ask her to marry him. His main concern was her father. No matter what Andrew had to offer it was nothing compared to the life she had lived as Edward Stratton's daughter. But true love went beyond mere possessions. Besides, his heart had already crossed the boundary. He pondered on the thought, then remembered the way Iris' face lit up when he came charging into the yard with the winning bid. He concluded just before sleep overtook him that Iris' heart had crossed the boundary too.

...

Iris was awakened by a crashing sound then hurried footsteps, followed by a shrill scream and a door slamming. In the dark she tumbled out of bed, struggling into her wrapper as she ran from her room calling for her aunt. She flew down the steps and was met by Stella who was bustling to the study where they heard the alarm in Emma's voice on the other side of the door.

"Edward!"

Iris rushed into the study and saw Hickory and her aunt kneeling over her father who was lying prostrate on the floor. Iris let out a disarming cry when she looked passed her aunt's shoulder and saw her father's red face and the veins pulsating in his neck. Stella caught her breath then muttered something in German and fled to the kitchen, returning promptly with a wet cloth. Despite Emma's efforts to calm him, Edward brushed her aside, struggling to his feet before he dropped disparagingly into a chair.

"Father! What's wrong?"

Speechless, Edward sat slump-shouldered with his head drooping on his chest.

Emma turned sharply. "Hickory! Hurry and get the doctor."

"The letter," Edward stammered.

Emma grabbed Hickory's arm. "As soon as you've spoken to Doctor Shelton take this letter to Mr. Harwick. Hurry!" Iris noticed that her aunt's face was drained of color when she looked up at Stella. "Go make some tea, and Iris, run and get a blanket."

Stella turned and scurried from the room while Iris groaned then fled, leaving behind a trail of unanswered questions. After Iris was gone Emma covered her pinched lips with her fingertips, her eyes closed tightly.

"Edward, please don't die," she moaned, the forbidden words lodged in her throat.

"Th...ey'll te...ll her," Edward muttered, his words slurring together.

Emma's eyes flew open like large round disks, full of uncertainty. Before she could reply, Edward pressed a clenched fist tightly into his chest.

"O...on th...waw," the words stumbled out of Edward's mouth. "..vy on...on...th...the...wa..."

"What are you trying to say?" Terrified, Emma's hands clutched at her throat. Edward struggled to get up. It was all Emma could do to hold him down when Iris rushed into the room and to her father's side. Fighting back the tears that were already visible on her cheeks Iris pleaded with her father.

"Father, lay down over here," she spoke slowly and patiently. "Here, we'll help you."

Together, the two women edged the big man across the room to a couch with overstuffed cushions. "Don't worry, everything's going to be all right, Father," Iris spoke calmly.

"Ir..is, on...the...waw...I...vy." Edward's words slurred together. It was impossible for Iris to understand what he was saying.

"I'm right here, Father. I'm not going anywhere."

...

"He's had a mild stroke," Doctor Shelton said returning the stethoscope to his bag. "His right side is slightly paralyzed but it won't be permanent. In time he'll come around."

"Why is he having such a hard time speaking?" Iris fought the painful lump in her throat; her heart was near to bursting.

"It's merely a side effect of the stroke. It won't last long," the doctor replied as he positioned his hat. "I'm afraid it will take a great deal of patience on both your parts to work with him, since he won't be able to communicate very well. As soon as he's well enough to sit up, give him a pencil and paper and he may be able to jot down a few words."

"I'll sit with him tonight," Iris quickly volunteered.

"You can do that if you like, but all you'll be doing, young lady, is wearing yourself out. The main thing that will help is proper care, bed rest, and time. I'll be leaving some sleeping draught in case he becomes overly agitated. The instructions are on the bottle. You may find it helpful yourself should you become overly distressed and are unable to sleep." Doctor Shelton set a brown bottle on the bedside table and started toward the door. "Reading would keep his mind stimulated, and soothing conversation can be quite uplifting."

Emma and Iris dumbfounded stared at the doctor, who remained calmly unaffected by the tragedy.

"Don't look so downhearted. Edward is quite fortunate. Most men who suffer from strokes die before the doctor even arrives, or they never fully recover. I feel very confident about this. He'll recover nicely, but I assure you, it won't happen overnight."

Accustomed to the shocked state of family members, the doctor dismissed himself. Emma and Iris didn't say a word until they heard the front door shut.

"Well, I guess we have our assignments," Emma said with

as much confidence as she could muster.

"I can sit up with father, can't I?" Iris looked worriedly at her aunt.

"Just for awhile. I'm afraid two sick people on my hands would be a bit much for me to handle."

They embraced and Iris kissed her aunt's cheek. "He'll be all right won't he Aunt Emma?"

"I have complete trust in Doctor Shelton, Iris. If he says your father will be all right then I'm sure he will. Now try to get some sleep, Iris. I want you to go over to the Stevens' tomorrow and tell Jacob about your father. There's some things we'll be needing help with and I'll need his advice."

Iris smiled, happy that her Aunt asked her to go to the Stevens' place instead of asking Hickory or one of the hands. It would give her the opportunity to see Andrew again.

CHAPTER FIFTEEN

The next morning, bright and early, there was a knock on the front door at the Stratton's house. Emma was surprised to see a nicely dressed middle aged man who promptly removed his black homburg hat and nodded a simple greeting.

"Good morning. My name is Brenton Hadley and I'm here to see Mr. Stratton concerning a letter that was left at Mr. Harwick's office late last night."

"We were expecting Mr. Harwick," Emma commented.

"I'm Mr. Harwick's assistant." Brenton paused, a frown making its way across his brow as he adjusted his round wire-rimmed glasses. "I know that you weren't expecting me, Mrs. Stratton, but Mr. Harwick is out of town, and since your husband's letter appeared quite urgent I thought it best to respond immediately."

Emma tried not to smile but Mr. Hadley's obvious disquietude caused her to feel sorry for him. To put him at ease she quickly extended her hand. "There is no Mrs. Stratton. I'm Edward's sister, Emma Stratton. Won't you please come in."

"I'm sorry," Brenton cordially apologized.

"There's no need to apologize, Mr. Hadley, it's happened before," Emma kindly smiled. "May I take your hat?"

When Brenton's shoulders relaxed, Emma couldn't help but notice how nicely they shaped his black coat. "You must be new in town. I don't recall Edward having ever mentioned your name."

"I'm somewhat of a newcomer. I've only been here for two months," Brenton answered, his soft blue eyes fixed attentively on Emma.

Emma noted his careful manner that was certainly different from any of the farmers with whom Edward had dealings. She set his hat on a side table. His unexpected presence was a pleasant, though unsettling change, one, she quickly concluded, she would probably never see again. She suddenly caught her breath, not realizing that she was holding it during her quick assessment.

"I'm afraid Mr. Stratton won't be able to see you this morning Mr. Hadley. If you'll have a seat in the parlor I'll ask Stella to bring us some coffee. There's a few things that need some explaining." Without thinking to open the drapes Emma left Mr. Hadley sitting in the dim parlor. Not until she returned from the brightly lit kitchen did she realize her mistake.

"I'm so sorry, Mr. Hadley," Emma shook her head while fluttering from one window to the next drawing back the long panels. "I wasn't thinking. I usually leave the drapes closed to keep the room cool and, well, I was just coming downstairs when you knocked."

Brenton crossed his leg and patted his hand resting on his knee. "I was rather enjoying the dim solitude. It's a refreshing change from my usual hectic pace."

Emma turned away from the last window. "I can leave these closed if you like."

"That would be fine," Brenton said just as Stella appeared, carrying a tray with steaming coffee and a small plate with biscuits and jelly.

"Over there, Stella," Emma instructed just before she sat down on an occasional chair, done in needlework, a few feet from Mr. Hadley.

The couple watched quietly as the cook set the tray down and carefully arranged the silverware. Emma slightly nodded at Stella. "Thank you, that'll be all for now."

As Stella shuffled away, Emma motioned toward the table. "We were just getting ready to have breakfast when you arrived. Would you like an egg or some...?"

"No, thank you. A cup of coffee will be fine."

"Please help yourself," Emma nodded toward the tray.

Brenton picked up the saucer, careful to balance the cup as he brought it to his lips. "You mentioned earlier that Mr. Stratton wouldn't be joining us," he said before he took a steamy gulp.

"That's what I need to talk to you about before my niece

comes downstairs. It is of utmost importance, Mr. Hadley, that what I am about to tell you go no further than this room."

...

Iris had just put on her pink nainsook day dress and tied her hair back and was starting down the stairs when she heard voices in the parlor. Wondering who would be paying her aunt a visit this early in the morning, she looked out one of the side windows but failed to recognize the polished black buggy or the striking chestnut mare. She turned around and frowned, fighting the desperate urge to knock on the door. At least it wasn't that detestable Leo Branson. Then she heard her aunt's voice sounding unusually strained.

"He's not sure, but he's afraid they've gone to search for her."

"Will she come back then?" An unfamiliar voice questioned.

"I don't think so," her aunt replied in a stilted tone.

"It sounds like they're trying to blackmail him," the man stated.

"It's possible but..."

"Iris! What are you up to now?"

Iris jumped at the sound of Stella's gruff reprimand. She whirled around and stumbled back against the door and the conversation in the parlor stopped abruptly.

"I...I was..."

The door opened and Emma slipped out of the room, holding the door shut behind her. "Iris! What's all this commotion I hear?"

"I...I...nothing." Iris frowned slightly at Stella's coarse look of disapproval. She looked back at her aunt. "I was just coming down to breakfast when I heard you talking in the parlor. I didn't know that we had a visitor."

"You really should be more careful, Iris. One of these days you're going to hurt yourself tromping around the way you do." Emma lightly touched Iris' arm then turned to face the door.

"That will be all for now, Stella," she said over her shoulder. "Iris, I want you to meet someone."

Iris reluctantly followed her aunt into the parlor, thankful that it was dim enough to hide the flustered look on her face. She didn't really feel like meeting anyone. When her aunt shut the door and stepped into the room, Iris was surprised to see a handsome, most distinguished looking man standing across the room. He wasn't at all what she had expected.

"Iris, this is Mr. Hadley. He's Mr. Harwick's assistant. You remember Mr. Harwick, your father's solicitor. Mr. Hadley this is my niece, Iris Stratton."

In two long strides Mr. Hadley was across the room with his hand outstretched. "It's nice to meet you, Miss Stratton. I was just talking to your aunt about your father's unfortunate setback. I hope that he will be feeling better soon."

"Thank you, Mr. Hadley. The doctor's reassured us that it will just take time."

"Would you like to join us, Iris?" Emma moved toward the breakfast tray. "We were just having some coffee and biscuits."

Iris shook her head. "No, thank you. I'll get something in the kitchen. I want to read to father before I go over to the Stevens'."

"I want you to go after lunch, Iris. This morning you need to trim the roses for your father."

Brenton started toward the door. "Don't let me keep you. I really have all the information Mr. Harwick will need for now. There's not much else we can do until we talk to Mr. Stratton."

Emma opened the parlor door and stepped into the hall and Mr. Hadley followed her to the front door.

Iris guardedly watched her aunt and Mr. Hadley exchange smiles. Her aunt was fumbling with the lace on her collar and it definitely appeared as if she was trying hard not to look directly at Mr. Hadley. Iris never saw her aunt act self conscious before. She looked at Mr. Hadley to see if he was uneasy but he appeared calm, almost charmed by the light blush that suddenly appeared on her aunt's cheeks. Iris was growing quite amused at how wildly romantic they were acting.

Emma handed Mr. Hadley his hat. "Feel free to come back any time," she said meekly as she opened the door.

Arranging his glasses, Mr. Hadley nodded. "Hopefully I'll be able to talk with Mr. Stratton soon. In the meantime assure him that there's nothing to worry about. Ladies," he said, tipping his hat briefly.

Iris was shocked when her aunt readily offered her hand to Mr. Hadley.

"It was nice to meet you, Mr. Hadley. You've been a great deal of help and comfort."

With his lips pressed firmly together Mr. Hadley smiled back. "I'm more than glad to be of assistance."

The couple stepped onto the porch and Iris stood near the open door. She smiled; happy with how charming her aunt and Mr. Hadley looked. It was like viewing two long lost friends parting as Mr. Hadley awkwardly descended the steps and climbed into the buggy. Even after he was headed down the road, disappearing like an afterthought, her aunt stood watching him.

"Aunt Emma?" Iris looked curiously at her aunt who obviously didn't hear a word she said.

"What?" Emma started. "What did you say, Iris?"

Iris looked down the road where only a cloud of dust remained. "What was that man here for? Is something wrong?"

"His name is Mr. Hadley, Iris, and he was here because of the letter your father sent last night."

"Was it about Mr. Branson?" Iris asked hopefully.

"Yes...yes it was," Emma said turning to go inside. "There's nothing to worry about. Mr. Hadley will contact Mr. Harwick and they'll take care of everything until your father's feeling better."

"Does he know where the Bransons went?"

"No, dear, I don't think so," Emma replied.

"When they come back will he send them a letter telling

them not to come here anymore?" Iris wrung her hands at her waist. "It's their fault that father's ill."

"I told you there's nothing to worry about. Mr. Hadley seems to be very capable." Emma assured her.

Iris followed her aunt into the house. "Have you ever met Mr. Hadley before?"

"Whatever gave you that idea?" Emma went into the parlor and began closing the drapes.

"I just wondered," Iris smiled in the shadows. "I guess I'll go see if fathers awake yet."

Without turning around Emma said, "if he is, then call down the stairs so Stella can bring a tray up for him."

CHAPTER SIXTEEN

'I once loved the prairie...'

Iris carefully made her way up the attic steps thinking her father might like it if she read 'Camelot' to him. She hated to think of books collecting dust and turning brittle in the dark. Maybe they were already too old and frail to handle, but she had to try. They used to belong to her mother. Hopefully, they would cheer up her father. She willed herself not to look at anything else. It would only make her upset. No one seemed ready or willing to offer her more than simple answers to perplexing questions. The thought suddenly reminded her of what she overheard her aunt say to Mr. Hadley in the parlor. She definitely said, 'He's afraid they've gone to search for her.' And Mr. Hadley had asked, 'Will she come back then?' Iris wondered who they were talking about. No one they knew had gone away and was expected to return. She picked up the book she was looking for and blew the dust off the cover. It must be one of Mr. Harwick's clients. Maybe Mr. Harwick was searching for her and that's why he wasn't available. Whatever it was, Iris was certain Mr. Hadley lived an exciting life with many interesting stories to tell. It would be amusing, watching her aunt react to his storytelling.

After she left the attic, Iris bent over the banister and called downstairs to let Stella know that her father was awake. She fluttered into his room and dropped a little kiss on his cheek before she sat down with her hands folded on the book in her lap.

"You don't care if I read to you do you father?" Iris asked, hoping her father would try to answer her. But he never said a word. For a long time he stared at the wall opposite the bed. Iris opened the book and slowly started reading. The sound of her voice filled the room, one by one the words creating the picture of the magical land known as Camelot. A short time passed before Stella appeared at the door with a breakfast tray. She craned her neck to look at Edward whose eyes lit up when he saw her.

"Goot morning Mr. Stratton, you're looking much better dis morning." She looked sternly at Iris before she walked across the room and set the tray down. "Goot. Reading to your faddur will keep you out of mischief."

"What makes you think I was being mischievous?" Iris challenged.

"I know you. You are too curious for your own goot," Stella said with her arms crossed tightly over her chest.

Standing up, Iris' eyes sparkled as she picked up a spoon. "You aren't going to tell on me now are you Stella?"

"I shood. Your aunt expects you to act like a lady."

"I'll try, I promise." Iris' smile widened.

"You don't fool me. I see da fisty little girl in your eyes."

Iris' arm quickly encirled Stella's stout neck. "Thank you, Stella. I can always count on you to see the real me."

"Dat's not vhat I meant and you know it," Stella stiffened, trying hard to keep a stern face.

Iris held the spoon with her little finger poised in the air. "No matter how ladylike I'm forced to be, you see me as the carefree creature of nature that I really am."

Stella threw up her hands. "Ach! I give up." She shuffled toward the door. "You be a goot girl now and feed your faddur."

Feeding her father took more effort than Iris realized. She struggled to support his head with one hand while feeding him with the other, moving painstakingly slow so as not to rush him. He managed to swallow the broth she offered before he fell back against the pillows exhausted. Iris moved the tray and plopped back down, feeling quite worn out by the tedious process. Looking around the room, she picked up a newspaper lying on the tray and opened it, looking for something else to read when she came to the ladies page where she noticed a column of poetry. Scanning the words she read a poem entitled, 'The Dream' in an undertone.

"Oh, but that I were yours
and not a wisp
If love was real

not just a wish
and your very soul more to me
than a fleeting dream
my heart once kissed"

She whispered the name, Sloan, wondering who the author was, amazed at how effectively the words made her heart yearn for Andrew. She imagined her mother having such a deep longing for her father and she looked at him, lying quietly with his eyes closed. Suddenly it struck her, the fact that he might be like this for days or weeks, maybe...forever, never remembering love. With her lips pressed tightly together she forced herself not to think of the possibility. For a moment she listened to him breathing, hoping that sleep would heal him somehow.

Deciding to sit with him a while longer, she picked up the book again. He showed no reaction. She had imagined, as she so often did when she thought about her mother, that it had been a gift from her father and at some time her parents sat together reading the enchanting love story. She thumbed through the pages then opened it from the back when all at once she saw some hand writing. The ink had faded with time causing her to peer at the worn scrawling. She read the words in an undertone.

'I once loved the prairie, crowned by the vast blue sky, full of fleeting clouds. In the spring it is beautiful and tender. The wildflowers whisper poetry to the wind, playing a gentle song. In the summer the warm breeze is full of secrets carried across the land in whispering echoes of those who came before me. All too quickly I learned how deceiving this place can really be. It begins in the fall, even as your heart is surging toward the vibrancy around you, and your very being is caving into the magic weaving its way through the trees. One night a cold gust of wind sweeps across the great expanse tearing the beautiful tapestry before it blows away. The wind no longer comes in soft billows. It slowly creeps in from the north. Like a serpent seeking refuge it slithers across the lonely floors. It seeps into your skin searching through your soul until it finds just the right niche where it can chant its tormenting dirge, repeating it over and over again like a baby crying in the night. It never goes away. You finally succumb to...'

Iris slammed the book shut, her mind full of dark, confusing images. She quickly opened the cover and looked hard at her mother's name. The writing was the same. So much love and yet so much hate in those few sentences. It was hard for her to grasp such misery when she herself loved the prairie, no matter what emotion it stirred in her. She gathered a shaky breath and looked back at her father. Why had she never been told about her mother's feelings? She paused to consider. It had to be because her father never knew how her mother felt. He always spoke kindly of her. Never once had he mentioned her being so sad. Her aunt probably didn't know either, since she only knew her mother for a short while. Iris held the book against her chest as she stared at the picture of her mother on the wall. Though the words saddened her, it brought the past closer making her mother seem all the more real.

Iris spent the rest of the morning leisurely pruning the roses, their sweet scent causing her to think of poetry. She had lunch with her father, who remained quiet, unwilling to write his thoughts on the paper Iris offered.

"Iris! Rebecca's here," Her aunt's voice trailed up the steps.

Iris looked at her father who had fallen asleep. Quietly she left the room, and looking over the banister, she saw Rebecca standing by the door waiting for her. Iris noticed that she was wearing her riding pants. She was glad because she wanted to change out of her dress before she rode over to the Stevens'.

"Rebecca," she motioned for Rebecca to come upstairs. "Shh!" Iris touched her lips. "Father's asleep."

In her room, she was changing out of her dress when she turned to Rebecca who was sitting on the edge of the bed. "I haven't been riding for so long. I want to ride as far as the horizon and into tomorrow."

"Wouldn't that be fun," Rebecca said dreamily. "To be

able to ride into the future."

"Sometimes I wish I could ride into the past," Iris confessed.

"Are you worried about your father, Iris?" Rebecca asked, concerned when Iris began to talk about things that she couldn't change.

Iris was quiet for a moment before she shrugged. "I guess. The doctor thinks that he'll be all right though." She started to braid her hair. "I just don't like it that he can't say anything."

"Do you think he'll ever be like he was before?" Rebecca's eyes rested on Iris.

"I hope so," Iris replied. "He hasn't finished sketching the windmill yet."

"Then I know he'll be all right," Rebecca said encouragingly. "You're father always finishes what he starts."

Iris thought about what she had read in the book and wondered what Rebecca would think of her mother if she knew that she had given up on the prairie. "Does your mother like living here?" she asked absently.

"What?" Rebecca looked surprised. "I don't really know. She's never said anything about it."

"Read this," Iris picked up the book from her dresser and handed it to Rebecca. "Just read the last page."

Rebecca carefully turned the yellowed pages. "Where did you get this?"

"In the attic. Just read what it says, right there," Iris pointed to the writing.

The room filled with silence as Rebecca's eyes followed Lydia's thoughts across the page. She closed the book and looked at Iris, her eyes full of wonder. "It's beautiful. Who wrote it?"

"My mother," Iris said in a distant voice. She sat down on the bed, holding the book carefully against her chest. "What do you think happened to change her?"

"I don't know. Mama once told me that some people can't stand wide open places. They feel lost." Rebecca thought for a moment. "Your mother was from Boston...maybe she missed her family, or..."

"Aunt Emma said she once lost a baby...a boy."

"Do you think that's when it happened?" Rebecca ventured.

"I don't know how old she was or what year it was," Iris said.

"Maybe you can ask your aunt," Rebecca suggested.

"I've asked her questions and she always says father will tell me the answers someday." Iris got up and put the book back on the dresser.

"That's all the more reason for him to get better." Rebecca went to the door then smiled back at Iris. "Come on Iris, let's go. And promise me you'll be happy for the rest of the day."

Iris smiled. "I promise."

"We can ride as fast as we want to. I want you to tell me everything Andrew said to you at the picnic, and...Well I have something to tell you too."

As soon as Hickory saddled Honey, the girls galloped off into the wind, leaving Emma standing on the porch shaking her head with motherly concern. If only Iris would wear the riding habit she had brought from Boston instead of those coarse britches and her father's shirts. Emma turned to go inside the house, thankful that at least Iris wasn't fretting overmuch about her father.

...

Iris and Rebecca raced down the road the way they always did ever since they were little girls on their first ponies. When they got to the branch hanging over the road they hauled their reins back at exactly the same time.

"We tied!" Rebecca exclaimed.

"I can never beat you, Rebecca Archer," Iris cried, all out of breath.

"Yes you have. Remember the time when..."

"Oh, that was so long ago. We were still wearing pigtails

then." Iris laughed when she thought how funny they used to look with their hair pulled back in tight braids and a few of their teeth missing.

"Let's climb the tree like we used to." Rebecca swung out of her saddle and was starting up the tree before Iris even had a chance to protest.

Iris followed Rebecca up the tree. "I can't believe we're doing this," she laughed.

When the two girls were sitting side by side looking out over the prairie, Rebecca laced her arm through Iris' and took in a deep breath. "Isn't it beautiful?"

"It's just like my mother wrote," Iris mused.

They silently took in the view, listening to the trill of the birds in the blowing grass before Rebecca sat up. "Iris, I have a surprise to tell you."

"I bet I know what it is." Iris smiled with her head bent to one side.

"What is it then?" Rebecca insisted.

"Todd kissed you at the picnic," Iris stated without hesitation.

Rebecca laughed. "Yes, but there's something else. When Iris couldn't guess Rebecca clasped her hands together. "Todd asked me to marry him."

Iris' eyes slowly grew wide with disbelief. "You're fooling me," she said, quickly assessing any change that might appear on Rebecca's face.

Rebecca simply shook her head. "He asked me last night, on the way home. And guess what else? He's riding out to meet the horses with Andrew. Mr. Stevens hired him. He already paid him too."

Iris gathered a shaky breath and released it with a long sigh. "What are you going to do Rebecca?"

"Marry him of course," Rebecca said, bubbling over with excitement.

"What about your mother? She's going to have the baby

any day now."

"Don't you think I know that?" Rebecca snapped.

"Have you told your parents yet?" Iris asked, concerned at the sudden change in Rebecca's tone of voice.

"No! They don't have to know everything I do." Rebecca started to climb down the tree and Iris hurried after her.

"You're not going to tell them?" Iris was beginning to get worried.

"I wish I didn't even tell you!" Rebecca angrily retorted.

"Rebecca, that's not fair."

Rebecca whirled around, confronting Iris. "What's not fair is me taking care of my mother's children all of my life with no time left for myself."

The two girls stared at each other until finally Rebecca turned and started for her horse.

"Rebecca, wait! I'm sorry." Iris called after her, but Rebecca had already swept into the saddle and was charging down the road. Disappointed, Iris dropped her shoulders and groaned. "Why does everything have to go wrong all at the same time?" Honey tossed her head, blowing air through her nostrils and Iris petted her quivering muzzle. "Things aren't going too well are they, Honey? I guess I'll have to go over and apologize after I talk to Mr. Stevens."

CHAPTER SEVENTEEN

Iris walked Honey the rest of the way to the Stevens', not as eager as she was earlier in the day to visit with Andrew. As she approached the Stevens' farm, she noticed two people sitting on the front porch. Nearing the house, she recognized Andrew and waved. The woman who was sitting opposite him had to be Mr. Steven's cousin.

"Iris." Andrew descended the steps as she was dismounting. "I wasn't expecting to see you this morning."

The front door swung open and Jacob Stevens stepped onto the porch. "Hello young lady. How's your father this morning?"

"That's why I stopped by. Aunt Emma wants to talk to you when you have the time," Iris answered.

Andrew took the reins and wrapped them around the hitching post. "Is he going to be all right, Iris?"

Iris nodded. "He's resting. The doctor says it'll be some time before he's back to normal though."

"I was just getting ready to ride over there. Do you think he could stand some company?" Jacob asked as he adjusted his hat.

"Father always enjoys your company," Iris smiled, glad to see someone feeling chipper.

"Iris, I want you to meet my cousin, Victoria Bishop." Jacob extended his hand in invitation while at the same time a tall, well proportioned young lady stood up and smiled sweetly at her.

'Your cousin? Iris silently quailed. Victoria Bishop was certainly not an old spinster. She didn't look a day over twenty-one. Blonde curls set off her large turquoise eyes, highlighting the apricot glow on her cheeks. Seeing how elegantly dressed she was made Iris immediately feel out of place and her hand subconsciously met the row of buttons on the work shirt she was wearing. She couldn't help but wonder what 'Victoria' did to make her bosom look so round and full. Probably stuffed her corset with handkerchiefs. Iris forced herself to blink though she still held her breath causing her face to pale. She had never seen a woman wear a dress like that in the middle of the afternoon...or at any time for that matter.

"Victoria, this is Iris Stratton. She's Edward's daughter. You've heard me speak of Edward Stratton."

Victoria walked slowly, taking small, precise steps until she reached the end of the porch where she gasped in ladylike surprise. "Oh! Why, yes, isn't he one of the farmers that lives down the road?" She spoke with a practiced lilt that made her voice sound artificial.

Iris hoped that no one saw her jaw twitch when she swallowed back her sudden hostility. She let her breath out slowly. "Yes, he is," she returned with as much calm as she could muster under the circumstance.

"Her father owns one of the largest farms in the county," Andrew was quick to add. "Some of the most beautiful country around."

"I can only imagine," Victoria looked toward the spanning horizon. "I've never seen so much lush farmland." She glanced coquettishly at Andrew who was staring at the fields that she had so aptly described. "Perhaps you would like to show me the countryside while I'm here Mr. Burgess."

Andrew's head popped up. "Well..." He looked at Mr. Stevens who seemed more than pleased with the idea. "I...yes, it would be my pleasure."

Iris shuffled, and not knowing what to do with her trembling hands she shoved them into her hip pockets. She gazed at the charming figure that looked like a porcelain doll and forced a smile. Victoria sweetly smiled back.

"I brought some lemons with me and we were just getting ready to have us some lemonade while we finished our game of checkers." The words dripped from her pink lips like maple syrup. "You will sit and watch us play won't you, Miss Stratton?"

Before Iris could reply Jacob started tromping down the

wide steps. "If you won't be needing anything Victoria I think I'll head out over to the Strattons to check on Ed."

"You go on ahead, Jake. If I need anything I'm sure Ida or Andrew can help me out."

"All right then. I'll see you later this afternoon."

As soon as Jacob walked away, Victoria gathered her violet sprigged skirt and swished over to the chairs where she and Andrew had been sitting when Iris rode up. "Come on you two before it's too late to finish the game."

As much as she wanted to go home, Iris didn't want to leave Andrew there alone with Miss Victoria Bishop. She knew how to play checkers; she played them often with her father, or in the evening sitting on the front porch with Hickory. But Victoria had already plainly stated that Iris was to be an observer and not a competitor.

There was only room for two to sit up to the crate the checker board was balanced on, so Iris was forced to sit off to the side. After they were seated, Iris noticed the strong scent of wildflowers in the air. Trying not to appear conspicuous she breathed deeply then realized that it was Victoria who smelled like honeysuckle. All at once she saw Andrew nod at Victoria in that chivalrous manner he displayed so well as he kindly reminded her that it was her turn to make a move. More than willing, Victoria took her time. She straightened her back, the move effectively drawing attention to her corseted waist while her creamy white fingers toyed above the checkers with ladylike precision. After she finally moved her checker she giggled, her eyes fixed dreamily on Andrew.

"You can't jump me if I move there, can you?"

Her brows arched, Iris quickly looked at Andrew, wondering if he noted the inviting tone in Victoria Bishop's voice. She couldn't help but think how ruggedly handsome he looked. His shirt, the color of midnight blue was opened at the neck exposing the white front of his long johns that failed to hide a wild patch of auburn hair, the same curly hair that showed on his bare arms that were tanned from his rolled up sleeves down to his expansive hands. His eyes leveled with the brim of his Stetson set low enough on his brow to accentuate the masculine curve of his nose. Iris' eyes clouded. Who wears a hat to play checkers? He looked more handsome than he had a right to look.

And Victoria Bishop was more inviting than a spring day.

When Andrew leaned back in his chair, Iris noticed how his black trousers hugged his long extended legs and she was glad that she had decided to stay.

"I thought you knew how to play," Iris challenged Victoria.

With her hand placed daintily on her swelling bosom Victoria drew her shoulder back. "It never hurts to redefine the rules. In all the years I've been playing I've met up with some pretty tricky players."

'I bet you have,' Iris thought just when Andrew rejoined.

"They play by a strict set of rules out here."

"I'm glad to hear it Mr. Burgess," Victoria cooed before she heaved a breathless sigh and brushed a few straying wisps of hair from her face.

That's when Iris noticed that Victoria had on a pair of earbobs. She'd never seen earbobs like that before. They looked like colored glass carved into flowers.

"My but it's hot out here," Victoria's bosom heaved gently. "I can't wait till this evening. Hopefully a cool breeze will blow in."

With his elbow propped on his knee, Andrew's chin rested in his cupped palm while he studied the board.

"I hear you're from St. Louis," Iris sought to change the subject before Victoria decided to invite Andrew to sit with her on the porch after the sun went down.

Victoria considered for a moment then answered, I was. Now I'm going to San Francisco to open a boarding house."

"A boarding house?" Iris muttered.

Just then the door creaked open then flapped shut. "I did just what you told me to do," Ida said as she walked across the porch, balancing a tray with three glasses full of lemonade. "I hope it tastes all right."

"It'll be just fine," Victoria complimented, without appearing to do so.

They each took a glass then Ida looked at Andrew who was making his move. "Seems like tomorrow's never going to get here," she said.

There was the quick snapping sound of tapping checkers just before Victoria let out a squeal that could have called the pigs in from the next county. "I won!" she shrilled, her arms flailing at her sides. Ida fell against the door and Iris sprang to her feet while Andrew started, toppling over, the glass in his hand sailing into the yard. His hat spun to a standstill just beyond the porch railing before lemonade splattered his face.

"Andrew!" Iris was struggling to get past the crate, the tented checker board and the scattered checkers when all at once Victoria lunged forward and fell over Andrew, dabbing his face with a lace handkerchief.

Andrew didn't move fast enough to suit Iris. She turned and stormed off the porch. Andrew called her name but all she could hear was the sound of Victoria's tinkling laughter.

CHAPTER EIGHTEEN

If love was like a gentle whisper
you would be the breath in me.

A cloud of dust followed Iris into the yard just before she hauled back the reins and flew off of Honey's back. She charged onto the porch, failing to notice Doctor Shelton's horse and buggy sitting in front of the house.

"If that's what he wants he can have her!" she grumbled as she threw open the screen door and immediately clambered up the stairs headed for her room. "You can't jump me if I move here, can you Andrew?" Iris tossed her head, mimicking the cajoling lilt in Victoria Bishop's voice then huffed in disgust and slammed her bedroom door. As though suddenly stricken with a fit of madness she threw open the doors on her armoire and began tearing out clothes. "Where is it?" There was a slight knock on the door just before it opened and Aunt Emma peeked curiously inside.

"Iris, what's wrong?" She stepped into the room and shut the door. "What are you looking for?"

"Nothing," Iris replied curtly as she hurled clothing of every kind over her head. She turned around; and, plopping on the floor, she looked suspiciously at her aunt. "Why didn't you tell me that Mr. Stevens' cousin was coming?"

"I thought I... Well, I guess I never had the chance to say anything before your father fell ill. What with the dance and the Bransons and... Why? What happened?"

"Nothing." Iris' shoulders dropped with a heavy sigh before she shot up like a jack rabbit and started tearing clothes out of her trunk.

"I'm assuming that you met her today," Emma said with a hint of amusement in her voice.

"What makes you think that?" Iris' voice sounded muffled from inside the depths of the trunk.

Emma eyed the clothes on the floor with some skepticism.

Iris had never worn that frilled camisole, and she had only worn that petticoat twice since her father brought it home from a business trip in St. Louis. She had only worn that billowing plum colored faille once and... worsted stockings? Emma shook her head. Hair ribbons sailed over Iris' head like a colorful tail on a kite.

"If you'll tell me what you're looking for, maybe I can help you find it," Emma offered instead of answering Iris' question.

"I'll find it in a minute." A shoe clunked on the floor beside Iris. "How's Father doing?"

Emma lifted her brow while carefully folding her arms in front of her. "I suppose you saw Doctor Shelton's buggy when you came charging in."

A pair of ruffled pantaloons flew in the air, landing on top of the open armoire door just before Iris fell back, all out of breath. "Is he all right?" she asked, studying her aunt who was struggling to keep her composure.

Emma's hands came together at her waist. She nodded slightly. "The doctor just left. He said your father's color looks much better today, and that he will gradually get his strength back." Emma paused. "Iris, you've chosen an unusual time to sort through your clothes. I do hope that you'll be finished with the job before bed tonight."

"I will," Iris rapidly nodded, eager for her aunt to leave so she could continue her search.

"Mr. Hadley sent word that he would be stopping by this evening to check on your father. I invited him to stay for supper. Under the circumstances I think it best that you eat downstairs with us."

"But I wanted to eat with Father," Iris stated, thinking how unusual it was for her aunt to invite a strange man to supper.

"Stella can feed your father tonight," Emma insisted. "I want you to put on your blue and white voile before you come down to eat."

Iris' brave smile belied the whirl wind of mixed emotions inside of her. "All right," she said, peering under the dust ruffle on her bed.

"After supper you can sit with your father for awhile and work on your pillow slips."

Iris groaned under the bed. She hated to embroider about as much as she hated making cakes.

"How many times have I asked you not to groan like that Iris? It is most unlady-like," Emma informed.

Iris frowned. She wondered if her aunt would think showing off one's bosom was unlady-like, but decided to broach that subject another day.

"I'm sorry, Aunt Emma. But you know how much I hate to embroider."

"It's only fitting that every young lady has some needle work to display. I assure you, some day you'll be quite proud of your accomplishment."

There was a long pause when Iris thought her needle work would be cause for tactless conversation among her Aunt's friends, but said instead, "Will you ask Stella to heat some water for me? I'm going to go see father for a few minutes, then I'd like to take a bath."

Emma refrained from showing surprise. She didn't want to discourage any interest Iris chose to display toward proper grooming. "All right, dear, but try not to take too long. It's nearly four o'clock and supper will be ready by six."

Iris heard the door click shut and waited to see if it would open again. When it didn't, she crawled out from under the bed with her corset in her hand. At last!

...

It was the strangest of things. Iris strained to make out the words her father struggled to say, thinking he was trying to say something profound when in fact it sounded very much like he was saying, 'Ivy on the wall.'

She crossed the room to the window where a shaft of late

afternoon sunlight poured onto the floor. Parting the curtains she looked down at the rose garden.

"Are you worried about the roses, Father?" She looked at her father who lay propped against several pillows. His eyes seemed to brighten. "And the ivy?" she added. "It's still there, growing on the wall with the pink roses. They're blooming, and they're so beautiful. Can you smell them when a breeze blows through the window?" She sat down beside the bed. "I trimmed them for you this morning, so there's nothing to worry about."

Her father's eyes watered and Iris placed a gentle hand on his. "Tomorrow, I'll pick some for your room," she whispered. Seeing how tired he was she stood up, with his hand in hers. "Don't worry, Father, I'll make sure to look after the garden until you're up and around."

Edward managed to breathe a reply that sounded very much to Iris like the same words he had spoken earlier. She had never seen her father so overly concerned about the roses...or the ivy growing on the wall.

"Try to get some rest, Father. I'll be back after supper." Iris kissed her father lightly on his forehead just before she tiptoed out of the room and hurried downstairs.

From the moment Iris entered the kitchen, Stella eyed her suspiciously. "Vhat suddenly makes you vant to take a bat before supper?" she quizzed.

Iris closed the curtain separating the kitchen from the pantry where Stella had set the tub. Stepping into the scented water she willingly replied, "Aunt Emma wants me to change since we're having company tonight."

"Dat never mate a difference before," Stella countered.

Iris called out from behind the curtain. "Is the water warm yet? I'm ready to wash my hair."

"Humph," Stella frowned as she shuffled toward the stove.

"I guess I just decided to take your advice from this morning," Iris said, laughing. "Stella, you worry too much!"

"Ja. I guess I shood be tankful," Stella groaned as she bent over to set a pitcher of water on the floor just inside the curtain.

"Why?" Iris asked.

"Dat you're taking a bat instead of making anodder cake," She stated flatly.

Iris' head popped out of the parted curtain. "That's not funny!" she rallied. "Andrew loved my cake. He paid a whole ten dollars for it."

"He could'ant help it. He tinks he's in love," Stella rejoined.

Iris slumped down in the water. 'If he's so in love', she thought, 'why didn't he come after me instead of staying at the Stevens' with that... Victoria Bishop?' Iris took a deep breath and stood up. 'No!' She wasn't going to think about that woman! Let him stay over there looking like a lost hound dog if he wanted to. She had an interesting evening to look forward to. Mr. Hadley was coming over and she was prepared to watch her aunt's reaction to his every move.

She washed her hair, rinsing it in lavender water before she briskly dried it then brushed it to a luxurious shine. In her room, standing in front of a full length mirror, she reminded herself that she was doing all this primping to make her aunt happy. Iris had finally made up her mind. As much as she dreaded putting on her corset, she would wear the confounded thing if it would make her 'appear' more presentable. If nothing else, she was determined to prove to herself that she could be just as amiable as any lady from St. Louis.

Iris began the arduous task of struggling into the contraption. Sucking in her breath, she maneuvered her breasts in an attempt to fasten the corset down the front. The job accomplished, she released a heavy sigh and fell over on the bed to catch her breath.

She tried to picture herself looking like Jacob Stevens' cousin, acting prim and proper, saying all the expected niceties at just the right moment; but all she could think about was Andrew.

Was he listening intently to Victoria Bishop's life story the same way he had once listened to hers? Iris shuddered. Unable to bear the thought, she forced herself to get up and finish dressing.

...

Supper was over and still there was no word from Andrew. Listening to her Aunt and Mr. Hadley converse while they drank their coffee, Iris felt herself growing more distressed. Trying to distract herself, she covertly studied Mr. Hadley, wondering if it was his side-burns or the slight arch near the center of his nose, or maybe it was his ridged brow that her aunt found so charming. It could be the way his glasses made him look so studious. Whatever the reason, Aunt Emma was obviously taken by him. She didn't seem able to keep her eyes off of the man. Iris dropped her gaze and attempted to hide her smile, but her thoughts continued unbidden. She tried to picture her aunt married to Mr. Hadley when suddenly Mr. Hadley turned his head and their eyes met. She felt the heat rising in her cheeks and she offered a pleasant smile. That's what she deserved for letting her imagination get the best of her.

Turning to look at Emma, Mr. Hadley said, "I've taken the liberty of leaving a letter with the hired man in charge at the Branson farm." He set his cup and saucer down. "I strongly suggested that he send it to Leonard Branson immediately."

"Thank you, Mr. Hadley." Emma took a deep breath and let it out slowly, her eyes closed for a brief moment. "Edward will be so pleased, and relieved to know that we'll be safe while he's convalescing."

Brenton crossed his leg. "You may assure Mr. Stratton that the Bransons' have been informed of the legal action that will be taken against them should they appear on or near his property."

Comforted by Mr. Hadley's strong convictions, Iris allowed her thoughts to drift back to Andrew. The door opened and Katie appeared with a tray of small cakes which she set on the table between Aunt Emma and Mr. Hadley. Katie was just leaving the room when Iris vaguely heard her aunt mention dominos. Iris was busy reminding herself that Andrew was no doubt getting ready for the drive tomorrow. She groaned inwardly. What was there to do that was more important than saying good-bye to her? Unwilling to consider the many ploys Victoria might come up with to distract Andrew, Iris quickly dismissed the thought.

"Iris, Mr. Hadley has decided to stay and play dominos if you care to join us," Aunt Emma offered kindly.

Realizing that her aunt, having been raised according to the laws of strict propriety, would expect someone to remain as long as she had a gentleman caller, and knowing that Katie would 'stand guard' if she left the room, Iris stood up, her hands folded at her waist. "Thank you, but I think I'll sit with father for a while." She answered with as much confidence as she could, considering the trying emotions wrestling inside of her. Feeling a bitter swelling in her throat she forced a congenial smile.

"You will come down and say good-bye to Mr. Hadley before he leaves won't you?" her aunt queried.

Iris nodded briefly before her aunt reminded her to send Katie back into the room. Mr. Hadley rose when Iris excused herself. Appropriately, Iris turned to smile as she opened the door and Mr. Hadley responded by bowing slightly.

The door clicked shut and Iris hurried up the stairs, fighting back the angry tears that already burned her lashes. She couldn't bear to sit any longer and watch her aunt and Mr. Hadley fawning over each other while they pretended to play a meaningful game of dominos, when all she could think about was what kind of an enchanting game Victoria Bishop might be teaching Andrew. The tears poured from her eyes like water from a down spout. "Men!" she blubbered. "Are they all so gullible?"

CHAPTER NINETEEN

Iris closed her bedroom door and turned around, groaning at the unsightly mess that greeted her. Tugging on the sides of her corset she shifted her torso uncomfortably, scolding aloud, "I did this for you, Andrew Burgess!"

Grabbing a handful of clothes she threw them on the bed. "You'd think by now he'd feel at least some twinge of guilt and hurry over to apologize."

The more she thought about it, the angrier she got until finally she pulled her dress off, tossing it aside before she peeled herself out of the suffocating corset. "The least he could do is to admit how foolish he acted in front of that...that opportunist! Humph!"

Iris took a deep, much needed breath while struggling with the irate thoughts flashing through her mind. Andrew was probably so taken by Victoria's obvious charms that he didn't even realize what hit him. She grimaced while examining the contour of her breasts in the mirror. "That's the effect those kinds of women have on men," she contemplated while turning her head from side to side, her chin slightly tilted, the way she had seen Victoria do it. Iris frowned. Feeling dowdy by comparison she turned away from the mirror. Mentally continuing her assessment of the charming Victoria Bishop, Iris resolutely crossed the room where she rummaged through the mounds of clothing until she found her trinket box. She concluded that she was not, and would never be, the kind of 'Boston society lady' that Andrew was used to.

Throwing open the lid on her trinket box, Iris crossed the room to the window. "Before the 'lady' traipses off to San Francisco maybe you would like to give her some small object of your affection, Andrew Burgess." She tossed the contents through the parted curtains. "There! Give her that." Iris whirled around, grabbed her book of Tennyson poems and hurled it into the yard. "Don't forget to ask her if she likes to read poetry," she bellowed just before she plunked down on the edge of her bed.

A sour moment passed and the room began to pale. Glancing through the parted curtains, Iris noticed a few grey clouds gathering. She unexpectedly caught her breath. Hopefully it wasn't going to rain. No matter how angry she was at Andrew she still wanted to watch him drive the horses across the plains. Suddenly a thought struck her. How wonderful it would be if her father could be there too, with her, when the horses came in. Wearing only her camisole and a petticoat she dashed out the door like a leaf caught in the wind, sweeping down the hall and into her father's room. She dropped onto the chair beside his bed, her hands clasped under her chin.

"Oh, Father! I thought of the most wonderful thing ever!"

Iris watched her father's eyes light up; and, not able to contain her joy any longer, she fell to the edge of the bed with her face next to his.

"Wouldn't it be wonderful if you could watch the horses come in?" She waited for any sign that would tell her he was enthused about her idea. A scant smile crossed his face and she hurried on. "Mr. Hadley's downstairs with Aunt Emma. He's ... he's Mr. Harwick's assistant. I'll ask him if he can come back tomorrow and help Hickory carry you down to the wagon. Oh, it'll be so much fun! You'll get to go outside. You'll feel better then, I know you will."

Her father nodded briefly with tears in his eyes. He painstakingly reached out and took her hand and Iris felt the strength slowly returning in his grip. He eyed her assessing when all at once his eyes shifted to the wall across the room and he whispered coarsely, "Ivy...there...on...on the waw, be...behind Lydia."

Confused, Iris stared at the picture of her mother. Looking back at her father she stroked his hand. "Don't worry, Father, everything will be all right. I'll take care of you, I promise."

Iris stood up, patting her father's hand, "I'll be back. I'm going downstairs to talk to Mr. Hadley." She turned to leave then stopped, her hands folded excitedly under her chin. "I guess I'd better put my dress back on before I do anything." She giggled with her shoulders hugging her neck. "Aunt Emma will be so pleased with the idea. She doesn't know it yet, but my asking Mr. Hadley to come back tomorrow will be doing her a great favor."

...

When Andrew saw the black shiny buggy sitting in front of the Strattons' house he nudged his horse quietly toward a clump of shrubs and dismounted. He had no idea who was visiting, or how long they would be there, but he was determined to see Iris. There were a few things he had been meaning to say to her and he was bound and determined to speak his mind before he headed out with the rest of the drovers at dawn. Not that she didn't have a right to be angry. It seemed like ever since he arrived in Nebraska girls were clamoring for his attention, and he had to admit he acted pretty much like a smitten school boy, when in fact he was dumbfounded at their straight forwardness. Victoria Bishop's bold behavior was the icing on the cake. He'd seen her kind in Boston, but this wasn't Boston. The sooner Iris knew that he wasn't impressed the better.

Dismounting, he tied the reins to a bush. He was glad that he had waited until after dusk; otherwise he would look mighty suspicious standing under Iris' bedroom window. He bent over and sifted through the grass looking for some pebbles.

"You'd think there was a shortage of men around here the way some women fuss over a guy," he grumbled, pushing his hat off his forehead as he stepped back and lightly tossed a pebble at the window. "I've about had it with lemonade and checkers, and ruffles enough to smother a guy just in passing."

When Iris didn't appear, Andrew tossed another rock then whistled gently, which only caused his horse to neigh and paw the ground. "Shh!" He turned and motioned to his horse when he felt something crunch under his boot. He squatted down and in the grass at his feet there was a tiny bouquet of crushed violets, a

129

glove and the book of Tennyson's poems he had given to Iris last summer. He took off his hat and scratched his head then stood up and looked thoughtfully at the window.

"She sure moves fast once she makes up her mind."

There was a noise to the side of the house. Andrew repositioned his hat and quickly stepped back into the shadows.

...

Somewhere off in the fields a mourning dove cooed and its mate responded. Holding up the hem of her dress, Iris stepped lightly through the cool evening grass twinkling with fire flies. With her aunt and Mr. Hadley upstairs talking to her father this was her only opportunity to go outside and hunt for the contents of her trinket box.

She hadn't felt a bit of remorse for ridding herself of Andrew's possessions until she went downstairs to present her idea of taking her father to the ridge to watch the horses. Her aunt and Mr. Hadley were so pleased with the prospect and, it appeared to Iris, of the opportunity to see one another again that Iris was struck with a sudden dreadful feeling of loss. To make matters even worse her aunt suggested perhaps Andrew never stopped by because he had to be up way before dawn. Iris suddenly felt childish for not giving him a chance to defend himself. What if something dreadful happened tomorrow? Or worse yet, what if he never came back? There would be nothing left but a tattered memory of her rash actions. She knew that it would be impossible to find the violets or the button in the dark, but if she failed to recover the book it would be ruined by the morning dew and she would never forgive herself. She crept slowly through the dark, shuddering at the memory of her last encounter with Leo Branson. Thank goodness she didn't have to worry about him anymore.

She was bent over feeling through the grass when all at once a man's voice sounded behind her.

"Looking for this?"

Iris let out a cry and swung around; ready to flee when she fell against Andrew who had just stepped out of the shadows.

"Andrew!" She let out a sigh of relief, "you nearly scared the life out of me." She stepped back and looked at the outline of his face beneath the brim of his Stetson. "What are you doing out here in the dark?"

"Seems like I should be the one asking questions."

Iris huffed and started to grab for the book when Andrew quickly drew it back.

"So, this is your book," he said coyly.

Iris stood firm, her arms crossed, her feet rooted to the ground. "You know full well that it belongs to me. And if you're hiding my glove I want that back too."

"I was under the assumption that it was my glove," Andrew pretended to be puzzled.

"Not anymore," Iris asserted. "It's mine, and you'd better give it back to me, Andrew Burgess."

"What'll I get for it?" Andrew asked glibly.

In the dappled moonlight Iris caught a glimmer of Andrew's dazzling smile. He was enjoying teasing her. "I'm not that easily charmed Andrew Burgess, and you know it," she stated flatly, clamping her lips tightly together.

"I was hoping maybe I'd get a little kiss good-bye since I'll be leaving in a few hours."

Quickly her smile turned to a scowl. "You...you..." Unable to think of anything fitting to call him she growled angrily. "How dare you ask me for a kiss when you don't deserve one."

"Not even a little one on my cheek?" Andrew bargained.

Iris noticed how the faint light highlighted Andrew's broad shoulders stretched beneath the expanse of his hat brim and, avoiding the flutter inside her chest, she quickly turned her head. "You've had enough female attention today to last you a week," she chided.

For a minute, Andrew pretended not to know what Iris was talking about. "Now don't tell me that you're upset over some woman who has the mistaken notion that she's every man's heartbeat."

"I can only imagine how fast your heart was beating this afternoon," Iris rebounded.

Andrew smiled broadly and took off his hat, holding it loosely by the fold in the crown. "Well, you're right if you're talking about the way you looked with your hands shoved into the hip pockets of the britches you had on this afternoon."

Iris gasped, astounded at his frankness. "I only had those on because I was out riding with Rebecca."

"Then I'll have to remember to thank Rebecca for asking you," Andrew said cordially.

"I can't believe you said that," Iris squared her shoulders, the way her aunt would expect her to under the circumstance.

Andrew looked down at his hat. "What if I said, I love you Iris, would you believe that?"

Iris was stunned. When he said her name the way he did he sounded so lost, so in need of her presence that she couldn't stop her heart from melting. How could she actually turn around and leave him standing there alone, thinking that she was still mad at him?

"You do?" she asked sheepishly.

Andrew nodded briefly. "Yes," he remained calm, his voice full of thought. "I figured you were upset when you left so abrupt like; and since I'm not real good with poetry and...and the kind of words a lady likes to hear, I tore this out of the paper just to prove it to you."

He put his hat on then reached inside his breast pocket, and taking a step closer he handed a ragged-edged piece of newspaper to Iris, who reached for it like a person who'd been hypnotized. She studied it for a moment before she looked up at Andrew and asked quietly, "What does it say?"

"Here." Andrew shuffled in his pants pockets and pulled out a match stick. He struck it on the heel of his boot and a circle of light glowed between them, highlighting the look of tender surprise on both of their faces when their eyes met. "You can read it, if you want to," Andrew said in a husky whisper. "But you better hurry before the light goes out."

Iris caught her breath then quickly read the words in a soft undertone.

Love's Silent Song

If love was like a gentle whisper
you would be the breath in me
If love was like a gentle verse
you would be my song
If love could draw our hearts together
it would happen secretly
Like the gentle breeze of early dawn

author unknown

Iris let out a short breath. "Oh, Andrew, that's beautiful. Who do you suppose wrote it?"

Andrew tossed the match onto the ground and snuffed it with the tip of his boot. "Hopefully it was someone who was loved and not someone in search of love."

"I think it was a woman waiting for the man she loved to come back to her," Iris said meditatively. "I think her name should be Sylvia."

"I like that name," Andrew said. "But I don't think she wrote it for herself. I think she wrote it for us." He gently gripped Iris' shoulders. "I wanted to give that to you when I got back...when we...I mean when I could ask you proper like, you know in the parlor when we were both all dressed up and...well, I want to build a house for you, Iris, I mean for us...for when we get married...if you'll have me."

Iris let out a little cry just before Andrew scooped her into his arms and kissed her rapaciously. Nothing mattered to her in all the world at that moment but the reality of their love. After a breathless moment Andrew's kiss trailed from her warm trembling lips to her face and down the length of her neck. Taking her face in the expanse of his hands he searched for meaning in the depth of her eyes.

"Do you love me, Iris?" he asked in a rough, shaky voice.

"Always," Iris breathed.

"Then you'll say yes?"

Andrew's eager words matched the beating of Iris' heart just before she drew back. Touching Andrew's face she felt his firm jaw and his lips that were still warm from their embrace, then the strength of his nose that led up over his defined cheeks to his enhanced brows. "Right now it's the only word I know." She formed the words against his lips, thus sealing the vow that was etching its way across both of their hearts.

Andrew reached into his hip pocket producing the glove, then picked up the book that he had dropped when he took Iris in his arms.

"Then you can have these back, and..." He dipped his hand into his shirt pocket. "Here's a button that fell out of the book. I figured it must be yours. But you can't have this until after tomorrow." He pulled the blue ribbon from around his neck and tucked it neatly into his breast pocket. Drawing Iris to his chest he spoke softly into her hair. "It'll be like you're right there with me, calling me home."

Iris tipped her head back and admired the shadowy outline of Andrew's features. The stars were beginning to wink in far off places and the sound of crickets filled the surrounding darkness. The windmill creaked and its long lattice silhouette reached out to them. Iris thought how magical the sky looked glittering overhead and how inviting the earth was, calling for them to build a home on the prairie. She promised herself that she would never forget this night or the way she felt engulfed in Andrew's arms.

"I'll be there, standing up on the ridge at the end of Stoney Creek Road. I'll wave when I see the horses coming."

"You won't be upset if I don't come by for a few days,

will you?" Andrew asked. "We'll be branding horses from sun up to sun down till the job's done."

Iris kissed his lips lightly. "I wish I could go with you."

"I'll be back, Iris. I promise."

"I'll be waiting for you," Iris said, her voice faltering before she added, "Kiss me again, Andrew."

He lifted her chin with his fingertips and again their lips met, refusing to part, each silently wanting more.

Iris finally drew back. "It's late, Andrew. You'll be so tired tomorrow you'll fall off your horse and I'll feel guilty for having kept you so long."

With his arms hanging loosely at his sides and his eyes filled with silent yearning, Andrew looked like a lost boy on the first day of school.

"I'll be back," he said with subdued emotion.

"You already said that," Iris reminded him.

His face set, Andrew turned his head to one side. "I guess I did. Well, I...I'd better go then." He turned toward his horse then stopped and looked at Iris who was standing in the shadows. "I really do love you, Iris, and I'm sorry about...about this afternoon. I..."

"Hurry and go Andrew, or you'll never come back." Iris' hands fluttered nervously in front of her face then clasped under her quivering chin. Andrew quickly mounted his horse, pulled the reins around, then galloped off into the darkness.

Iris' whole body trembled and her heart felt wonderfully swollen. She wanted to laugh and cry all in the same breath. She touched the button to her lips that yearned to be kissed again and again, then gathered her treasured possessions and turned away from the cloud of trailing dust that was just beginning to settle on the road.

CHAPTER TWENTY

Iris woke up the next morning, tingling from the memory of Andrew's strong arms surrounding her, her lips longing to be kissed again. Her arms stretched above her head. She yawned with her eyes closed envisioning herself as a hopeful bride and Andrew, as handsome as ever, her romantic cavalier. She reached for her book of poetry and flipped through the pages until she found the poem Andrew had given to her the night before. She read it twice then hugged it to her chest with a sigh.

"He loves me," she breathed.

Her mind flew to thoughts of her wedding day. There would be an abundance of flowers everywhere, baskets of rose petals for the children to toss, and garlands with tiny rosebuds weaved into streamers. Her aunt would order her the most fashionable gown, one in which she would simply disappear amidst yards of soft white satin edged in lace. The fitted bodice would be decorated in a floral pattern with hundreds of seed pearls. She would be transformed into a beautiful Bostonian lady, the kind her aunt used to tell her about when she was a little girl. Though Iris disliked extreme fashions, she would go to great lengths to see her aunt's smile of approval on her wedding day, not to mention the look of hopeful delight it would bring to Andrew's face.

Iris knew that she would never be a real debutante, flirting with young men at cotillions and flaunting practiced social graces while smartly playing Bach on the piano, or astutely reciting love sonnets in French. But for once in her life she would sacrifice her wild and carefree spirit to propriety, allowing her aunt to relish in her dreams. Even though there would be no gaitered footmen to greet the guests or swans down sheets for weary ladies to nap upon it would be a gala celebration; one that would be talked about for a long time to come. The long cherished vermeil service would be polished, and the crystal would sparkle from the glow of the candles in the tiered candelabra on the glistening oak table prepared for the many wedding guests. The seldom used china would be placed beside napkins edged with Belgian lace that would serve to enhance the gleaming forks, knives and countless spoons for entrees too numerous to mention.

Iris sighed with sheer delight. Her life had always been, and would continue to be, different from her aunts and from the young ladies Andrew was no doubt accustomed to meeting; but she didn't care, and most important of all Andrew didn't care. He loved her the way she was.

A faint whiff of ham frying and coffee brewing found its way up the stairs where it mingled with the sunshine pouring through the parted curtains. Iris bounded out of bed, giddy with excitement, eager to greet the day and anxious to tell her aunt the wonderful news. But first she would cut some roses to put in her father's room. When the time was right she would tell him about her and Andrew's plans to marry. Maybe he would remember how much he loved her mother, and then hopefully his attitude toward Andrew would soften. She said a quick, silent prayer that her father would be well enough when the time came to walk her down the aisle.

Hurrying through breakfast amidst her aunt's mindful glances, Iris scurried, without her wide-brimmed hat, to the garden where she relished the sun on her turned up face. She was just slipping some ivy into the basket with the roses when she looked up and saw Rebecca coming toward her.

"Rebecca! I'm so glad so see you. I have the most wonderful news to tell you."

Rebecca stopped beside Iris and plucked a few rose buds. "Your aunt said you were picking some roses for your father. I hope he's feeling better."

Iris glanced at Rebecca and noticed the distraught set of her jaw and the way her lips seemed pinched together when she stopped talking. It appeared that Rebecca was avoiding looking at her on purpose.

"You're not still angry with me are you, Rebecca?" Iris asked carefully.

Rebecca shook her head, a little too quickly to suit Iris, but she decided not to pursue the subject. With the baby due any day, Rebecca had to do extra work at home. Iris didn't want to make matters worse by discussing their disagreement. Perhaps an apology would help.

"I'm sorry if I hurt your feelings," Iris said. "Aunt Emma's always telling me how I speak without thinking first."

Rebecca slipped a budding rose behind her ear and looked at Iris through flecks of sunlight. "I'm not angry, really. Now, tell me how your father's doing."

Iris smiled. "Much better. He can sit up now, and he's talking a little more, even though we can't always make out exactly what he's saying."

Rebecca quietly watched Iris arrange the flowers before she looked down at the cluster of roses in her hand. "You said you had some news to tell me."

Iris laid the flower snippers on a small bench beside her basket and hurriedly gathered Rebecca's hands in hers. Her unblinking eyes grew large with anticipation and her lips pressed together for a wistful moment. "Andrew asked me to marry him last night. I haven't told anyone else."

Iris saw a quick frown flash across Rebecca's brow before Rebecca swiftly turned her head at the sound of some birds fluttering in a nearby bush. "You said that he loved you all along, and you were right," Rebecca's voice trembled. "I'm happy for you, Iris. I..." She stopped abruptly, lowering her head.

Drawing Rebecca's hands nearer, Iris sought her eyes. "Rebecca, what's wrong? And don't say nothing. I know that something's wrong."

"I'd...I'd hoped that you'd be as happy for Todd and me."

"Rebecca, you know that I am. I...I was just concerned, that's all, and, well, maybe I said it wrong. I didn't mean to. I said I was sorry."

"I know," Rebecca said sheepishly.

"You believe me, don't you? I wouldn't do or say anything on purpose to hurt your feelings."

Rebecca nodded rapidly. "Then you understand how I feel?" she asked in a low voice.

"I know it's been hard for you, having to help so much at home and all. You deserve to be happy, Rebecca."

"I wish my parents felt the same way."

"Have you told them yet?" Iris asked.

Rebecca shook her head, "No. Mother hasn't been feeling well, and...well, Father thinks Todd's too young. If I bring up the subject now it would just cause an argument."

"Maybe you can talk to them later after the..."

Rebecca quickly drew back her hands and shoved them into her pockets. "I don't think I'll be able to watch the horses with you like I said I would," she interrupted.

Iris couldn't help but notice how hard Rebecca fought to hide the edginess in her voice. Her own voice trembled when she asked, "Why not?"

Rebecca swept a trembling hand through her hair, gathering it on one side where she held it for a moment before she let it go. "I just can't that's all. I...I really should be going." She turned abruptly and started walking away. "I didn't tell anyone that I was leaving," she said over her shoulder, "and they'll be looking for me. There's so much to do before the baby comes."

"Is your mother all right?" Iris thought to ask.

"Yes. Just tired, and anxious for the baby to come," Rebecca replied.

"I can help if you want me to," Iris responded quickly.

Rebecca turned her head away. "No, that's okay."

Iris frowned then quickly raised her hand as if to stop Rebecca from leaving. "You'll let me know if you change your mind won't you?" she called out.

"Good-bye, Iris." Rebecca hurried away.

Iris' shoulders fell with a heavy sigh. She had so anticipated them watching the horses together. Disappointed, she took a deep breath and reached for the snippers. At least her father would be there.

Iris went into the house where she found her aunt in the kitchen preparing a bath for her father. Emma looked up when Iris came into the room.

"Where's Rebecca?" she asked, the concern showing on her face.

Iris shrugged as she set the basket of flowers on the table. "She left."

Emma was taken aback. "Left? Where did she go?"

"Home, I guess." Iris reached in the cupboard for a vase and began pouring water into it from a pitcher that her aunt used for watering the house plants.

"Is something wrong, Iris?"

"I asked her if everything was all right and she said everything was fine, her mother's been tired that's all."

"She didn't stay very long. What did she come over for?"

Sitting on a chair next to the table, Iris began to separate the flowers. "She just wanted to tell me that she wouldn't be able to go with us to watch the horses come in. She had to get home right away."

"I wonder if I should pay her mother a visit?"

Iris looked at her aunt who was pouring hot water into a blue speckled wash basin. "I offered to go over there, but Rebecca said they didn't need any help."

"I guess I'll wait then until Beth has the baby." Emma paused. "Remember, Mr. Hadley's coming by this afternoon," she added.

Iris smiled at the faint blush that turned her aunt's cheeks pink. Emma set the kettle of water back on the stove. "He won't be here until four o'clock. We'll be having supper a little early this evening." She gathered the length of huck toweling. "Stella's out in the garden snipping some chives to add to the soup she's been preparing for us to take over to the Stevens for when the men come in. I wonder if we should stop by and see how Beth's doing on our way back."

Iris stood up with the vase in her hand. "I don't think there's anything to worry about. I'm sure they'll send for you when the time comes."

"It's the neighborly thing to do, Iris. You've been taught that since you were a child."

A scowl set between Iris' brows. She didn't want to go over to the Stevens where she would be forced to sit and speak politely to Victoria Bishop, and after talking to Rebecca she didn't feel much like confronting her either. All she cared about at the moment was talking about Andrew.

"Why do we have to take the food over? Can't Hickory take it?"

"That wouldn't be polite, dear, and you know it." Aunt Emma picked up a bar of soap sitting on the table. "Don't scowl, Iris. You'll get wrinkles. Mr. Stevens has been very kind to us since your father's illness. It's only right that we show our support after the men came all this way with the horses. Besides, it's only proper that I pay a visit to Miss Bishop, to introduce myself."

Emma turned to leave then stopped and cast a curious glance at the flowers Iris was carrying. "What made you think to put ivy in with the flowers?"

"Father seems worried about the ivy. I think he's afraid that it'll die out. I just wanted him to see how well it's growing."

Emma's lips pursed for a brief moment. "If he's worried...oh, well, I suppose it's for the best." She started to walk away when Iris stopped her.

"Aunt Emma, I wanted..." Iris caught her breath. It just didn't seem the right time to tell her the news.

"What is it, Iris? I really must attend to your father before it gets too late. I would like us to make it over to the Stevens before lunch."

"Nothing, I...I'll just talk to you later."

"Are you sure?" Emma hesitated. "Is something else

bothering you?"

"I was worried about what to say in...in front of Victoria that's all." Iris felt comfortable with the half truth.

Emma walked over to Iris and hugged her cheek briefly. "Just be yourself, dear. When you put your mind to it, you're as amiable a young lady as any I grew up with in Boston. My mother always said, 'What the mind doesn't imagine the heart can't grieve over.'"

Iris' smile was warmed by a blush. How many times had she heard those words? She could always count on her aunt to console her, even when the occasion didn't call for it.

Emma walked away, her steps brisk and attentive. She called over her shoulder, "Don't wander off. As soon as I've attended to your father, we need to work on our crocheting. We should see to it before we leave for the Stevens."

Iris looked at the flowers, failing to erase the frown of disapproval from her brow. A trailing vine of ivy slipped over the edge of the vase and dropped to the floor and suddenly, as though a cold draft swept through the room, Iris shuddered, the expression falling from her face. She dazedly stared at the ivy while telling herself that she hadn't imagined it. Her aunt was visibly shaken when she mentioned the ivy growing on the wall.

CHAPTER TWENTY-ONE

After she had given Edward his bath Emma checked on Stella, who was working heartily in the kitchen. Offering an encouraging smile of approval, Emma then headed toward the parlor. When the parlor door opened Iris could hear Stella chattering at Katie, who had been busy all morning baking bread to take over to the Stevens. Iris had just taken out her crochet basket and was positioning herself near the lighted window when her aunt sat opposite her.

"Why do you suppose Father is so concerned about the roses, and the ivy?" Iris asked prudently.

"I don't really know, dear," Aunt Emma replied evasively, which indicated to Iris that something was definitely being kept from her; something more than her father's brief concern over the roses he had planted for her mother so many years ago.

"Yesterday, Father seemed concerned about the picture of Mother hanging on his bedroom wall. He said something about some ivy on the wall behind Lydia."

Emma gasped, quickly glancing at Iris while holding her finger to her mouth as though she had pricked herself. Suddenly her stunned expression vanished and her gaze dropped to the crocheting in her lap.

Iris looked worriedly at her aunt, who was sitting uncommonly stooped shouldered in obvious consternation. "Did I say something wrong?" she asked, puzzled.

"No. I...I was just surprised to hear that you're...your father was talking so much."

Iris remained silent. Whatever the secret was, it was too tragic or too painful for her father, or her aunt to discuss openly. Perhaps it had something to do with her mother, which suddenly led Iris to wonder why her father kept all her mother's belongings in the dusty attic. Her aunt had said that someday her father would tell her everything. Her insides cringed at the thought of some deep, dark mystery lingering, not only in the attic, but in her father's heart as well. Iris fidgeted uncomfortably. The thought was too disquieting to bear. She suddenly felt trapped, not only by the confines of the parlor, but by the ghostly secret that chose to haunt her at the most inopportune time.

"I hate crocheting," she blurted before realizing she had done so.

"Really, Iris, hate is hardly an appropriate term to apply to an activity that will, in the long run, benefit you greatly." Aunt Emma turned her eyes toward Iris, the sternness therein being reprimand enough. "Why, some of the most treasured heirlooms were patiently hand crafted by women such as you."

"I just want to go over to the Stevens now, and get it over with," Iris said despairingly.

"Practice patience, dear," Aunt Emma encouraged soberly. "You've only been crocheting for fifteen minutes. You'll never have your coverlet finished by the time you get married if you don't work faithfully at it."

Iris's eyes lit up. If she didn't know better she would insist that the secret she was forcing herself to hold back was written all over her face. Her aunt had surely deduced as much when she cast a disconcerted look in Iris's direction.

"What is it, Iris? I can tell when you're keeping something from me. Is it about Rebecca?"

Iris's shoulders hugged her neck as she fought to stifle an unexpected giggle. "No, it's about me, about Andrew and me."

"Yes," Emma said quietly.

"Andrew came by last night and..."

"When was he here?" Emma asked, her crocheting sitting idle in her lap.

"He came while you and Mr. Hadley were upstairs visiting with Father," Iris said, her eagerness mounting. "I...I dropped something out the window and when I went outside to look for it he...he was standing in the yard."

A perplexed look crossed over Emma's face. "He was just standing there?" she questioned.

146

"Well...yes. He came by to tell me that he would be heading out at dawn with the rest of the drovers. He just wanted to say good-bye. We talked for awhile, then...then he asked me to marry him."

Emma's shoulders abruptly set as straight and stiff as the back of the chair she was sitting on. "Oh, my!" she mildly exclaimed. "This poses somewhat of a problem."

"What?" Iris quizzed. "I don't see a problem. We're desperately in love."

"I'm afraid your father may see it in a different light," Emma propounded.

"Would he rather I marry that disgusting Leo Branson?" Iris said wryly.

"Of course not, and you know it. It's just that we know so little about Andrew Burgess."

"Do you really think John Stevens would consider choosing him as a partner; or that Mr. Stevens would allow him to work for him if he was the least bit irresponsible or careless?" Iris remained adamant.

"Of course not," Emma replied softly, "but a marriage proposal is quite another matter. It's not the same as...as well, horse wrangling."

Iris couldn't keep herself from giggling. "I'm sorry, Aunt Emma, I didn't mean to laugh, but that sounded so funny coming from you."

"I do know a bit about such matters," Emma said confidently.

"I know, but a wrangler can love someone just as true and lasting as a wealthy man with tenant farms. We'll just have to convince Father to see it that way."

"What do you mean; we'll have to convince him? I'm afraid, my dear, that it will take more than our convictions when it comes to the subject of you're getting married."

Iris bent slightly toward her aunt, her eyes imploring her. "You don't disagree, do you, Aunt Emma?" she gently pleaded.

"It's not up to me, Iris."

"But you do believe that I love him, don't you?" Iris continued to prod.

Her lashes laying gently on her cheeks, her lips pursed in thought, Emma seemed to be studying the needlework on her lap. She offered a belated smile. "Yes, I believe you Iris, and I want you to be happy; but, well...are you sure you're not being just a little bit impulsive?"

"No! I already told you that I've known since last summer that I loved Andrew, and I still do love him."

"I'm certain your father will think it's a bit reckless of you to make such a quick assessment."

Iris grimaced. "I've thought of nothing but our being together since Andrew left last summer to go back to Boston. I can't let him go away again."

Emma released a gentle sigh; one that Iris knew was appropriately suited for a lady under the circumstance. For the first time in her life, Iris saw a look of tender acceptance on her aunt's face, a look that she had never seen there before. Her aunt mumbled, "It is your nature to be somewhat impulsive. I'm sure your father will take that into consideration."

All at once Iris realized that her aunt was falling in love with Mr. Hadley. It was her own heart that Aunt Emma carefully challenged, for never in her life had she allowed her feelings to become impulsive and daring. Iris desperately wanted to embrace her lovingly, but she knew better. Her aunt would be mortified at the mere suggestion of her "catching a man's eye" at her age. Iris stifled her joy, knowing that it would happen in due course. Mr. Hadley would soon see the look of tender yearning that Iris saw now, and when that time came he wouldn't be able to help himself. He would fall hopelessly in love with the woman who thought love had passed her by.

...

A slight tap on the door interrupted the reflective silence. "Come in," Emma said, relieved when Stella appeared, drying her hands on a length of huck toweling.

"Da foud is ready to go," she announced.

"Thank you, Stella. If you'll send word with Katie, Hickory will carry the basket out to the buggie." Turning to Iris, Emma instructed, "If you're ready to leave then say good bye to your father and let's be on our way. We have a long day ahead of us."

Emma couldn't help but smile at the eager expression on her niece's face when Iris dropped her crocheting and flounced quickly out the door. She was so full of spirit that it almost pained Emma to have to insist she learn needlework. Emma gathered a quick breath, not realizing until she'd done so that she was feeling a bit shaky. A most unsettling feeling of joy and sorrow was flitting about inside her. It had much to do with Iris's announcement, but she knew that it had everything to do with her own unsteady emotions. She closed her eyes.

A wedding.

A brief overview of her past flashed into her mind. She saw herself as a young girl with the look of love in her eyes, the same look that made Iris' eyes sparkle when she spoke of Andrew. Emma's trembling fingers fluttered over her swollen lips and her eyes flew open. That was so long ago. She had almost forgotten that she was once hopelessly in love. Suddenly she thought of Mr. Hadley and she felt herself blushing. Could it be that she...? No. He had no doubt discerned that she was beyond capturing such a dream. Wide eyed, she searched the ceiling for an answer. Could she give her dream of having a beautiful wedding over to Iris? She gasped and her hands flew together in a tight clasp. She sprang to her feet, picked her crocheting up from off the floor, cast it hastily on the chair behind her and fled from the ghostly images of the past.

A short time later, listening to the sound of the horse's hooves on the road, Emma realized that her shadowy thoughts had followed her. She flicked the reins in an effort to dissuade them but the results were nil.

"I was once engaged to be married," she found herself saying aloud. When she realized that she had rapidly caught Iris' attention there was no turning the conversation about, so she proceeded delicately, inadvertently revealing that it was her feelings she was guarding and not the subject of Andrew's proposal to Iris.

"His name was Silas Dunn. My parents thought highly of him as he was quite a gentleman and spoken of with great respect in Boston society." Emma paused, allowing the sharp reeling images to flicker through her mind. "My mother came from a very distinguished family, one where the women traveled to Paris to purchase handmade Honiton or Belgian Duchesse lace along with the finest of silks and satins for their daughters' wedding gowns." She glanced briefly at Iris. "Cost meant little to women of society. All that seemed to matter was one's reputation." With her eyes fixed once again on the road she continued. "Every detail was publicized. My mother employed a French seamstress to fashion my gown. The veil of Brussels lace was specially designed by her milliner. The crown was of embroidered satin with seed pearls weaved throughout. It was then arrayed with countless yards of white billowing netting. Mother employed another embroiderer who worked many hours on a length of pearl satin that would eventually become the bodice for my dress. Overall it created a most beautiful motif."

Awe struck, Iris uttered, "I can't imagine wearing such finery."

Emma smiled. "That's the effect that was sought, a look so illusive any observer would feel as though he or she were in a dream. Ladies of society were expected to wear such wedding attire." Emma smiled faintly. "You can only imagine the feeling that swept through the groom when he beheld his bride."

"Do you still have the dress?" Iris asked hastily, and then apologized. "I'm sorry, I..."

Emma quickly touched Iris' hand. "Don't be sorry Iris. You have a right to ask after all these years. Actually, I should have told you sooner." There was a pause. Emma would tell her only what she had a right to say and no more. "No. It was sold to a dressmaker. I never married, Iris, because...well, when Silas Dunn discovered that I couldn't bare children he married a woman he had fallen in love with before he met me, a woman who had refused his initial proposal. All I have left is my veil that is now the curtain on the window in my room."

Iris gasped. Emma patted her hand then took a firm grip on the reins to steady her own emotions. "It was for the best, in the long run. I came to Nebraska to be with your father when...when his life changed, and as a result I have you." Emma glanced at Iris and smiled. "I've never regretted that decision Iris."

Before Iris could reply, Emma directed the buggy into the Stevens' yard and pulled gently on the reins. The door immediately opened and Ida appeared, waving, her face lit up with a smile. An older man came sauntering out of the barn, squinting into the sunlight. When he recognized the Stratton's buggy he at once set aside the small hand tools he was carrying and hurried to assist the ladies. Ida introduced him.

"This is Ned. He works in the tack room."

Emma smiled and thanked him before she asked if he would kindly carry the basket of food into the house. By then Ida had walked over to the buggy.

"Come in and have tea," she insisted.

"Thank you Ida, but I'm afraid we don't have time today," Emma apologized. "We thought we might stop at the Archer's to see how Beth is getting along, and then we have to get ready for tonight. We're going to try to take Mr. Stratton to the ridge this afternoon to watch the horses come in."

Ida smiled. "It will be a great event, like in the old days. It is good to watch the horses." She shook her head morosely. "I don't think it will ever happen again."

Emma liked the deep-seated feeling of belonging to the land that Ida emitted. It was a comforting, settled sort of feeling that everyone should experience. She smiled fondly then looked up at the house when the door padded shut and Ned started heading back to the barn. "Is Miss Bishop here?" she asked Ida. "I would like to meet her before all the commotion begins and I miss the opportunity."

Emma couldn't help but notice the frown on Ida's face before she turned and started back to the house. She motioned for Iris to follow and they had just reached the steps when the dark screen door screeched open and a sleepy-eyed, tousle haired woman appeared. Emma readily assumed that it was Victoria Bishop, for only a debutante, and one most assuredly from Boston, would wear such a stunning sleeping gown in the middle of the morning. Emma hadn't seen such sheer, lacey finery in years and her heart once again swelled with tangled memories.

The tall, willowy figure in the flowing, off the shoulder gown stepped lightly onto the porch before she stretched her long magnolia white arms and her swan-like neck, yawning as delicately and sweetly as a morning glory reaching toward the light. "Oh! I wasn't aware that we had company. You should have awakened me Ida."

Victoria breathed lightly and walked over to the edge of the porch. "What a glorious day." She whirled around and looked directly at Iris. "You should have been here this morning. It was like nothing I've ever seen before, watching the cowboys gathering at dawn. All those horses, and the way the men just got them to do whatever they wanted them to just by a flick of the reins." Her long feathery lashes swept down over her startling blue eyes as she rolled her head back onto her bare shoulder, her arms bent, her long splayed fingers sweeping back the length of her blonde hair that effectively caught the sunlight. "This country makes a person want to stay here forever. I've never seen the sun come up the way it did this morning."

"You've probably never seen the sun..."

"Go down like it does here either," Emma quickly interrupted Iris. "Well, it won't be long. The horses will be coming in before we know it, and there's so much to do before then."

Victoria whirled around to face Ida who stood with her arms crossed and her face set. "Ida! I hope you thought to offer the ladies some tea."

"Yes," Emma nodded diffidently. "She was most thoughtful, but we'll have to make it another time."

Victoria smiled graciously, drawing a deep breath as she glided over to a small draped table setting on the porch where she picked up a copy of Punch magazine and flipped leisurely through the pages. "I think I'll have some tea out here on the porch, Ida, and a slice of bread with some jam, and a poached egg." Ida frowned and reached for the knob on the screen door. "Now remember, don't cook the egg too long," Victoria instructed. Ida went inside and Victoria shook her head pertly. "I don't think she's ever made a poached egg. Where I come from the hired help don't eat like we do. They have their own way of doing things, but then everything's different out here. Don't you think so, Iris?"

"For someone like you it would take some getting used to," Iris quipped.

Emma's hands clasped tightly at her waist when she saw Iris smile wanly. She wondered for a quick moment where her niece has learned such bantering. Her hand automatically thrust forward. "It really has been a pleasure meeting you, Miss Bishop. I...we really should be leaving though, in order to get ready for tonight."

"You'll be here then?" Victoria looked surprised.

"We'll be the first to arrive," Iris remarked.

"I'll be sure to look for you," Victoria extended her hand to Emma. "And do come back when you can stay for tea."

Iris turned and abruptly started walking toward the buggy.

"Thank you, we'll do that," Emma replied in as steady a voice as she was able to manage. Emma had no sooner sat down and picked up the reins when Iris huffed despite Emma's muffled insistence that Victoria might hear her.

"I don't care!" Iris wailed.

Emma snapped the reins harder than she intended and the horse lunged forward.

Iris glared furiously ahead while tugging at her simple bodice. "I'm sure every 'cowboy' within fifty miles saw her this morning dressed in that...that..."

"Oh my," Emma muttered unawares. She hadn't considered the possibility until just then. After the horse had slowed to a steady trot Emma looked expectantly at Iris then squared her shoulders. With her chin set and her eyes fixed on the road straight ahead she stated, "Make sure you're there promptly to greet Andrew when he returns."

CHAPTER TWENTY-TWO

Dreams live on in the hearts of men...
Let me be your dream.

Little else was said the rest of the way home as Emma and Iris were caught up in their own disquieting thoughts. Emma stated that it would be best to forgo her intended visit with Beth Archer, concluding that she would be of little assistance, her nerves having been somewhat frayed by Miss Bishop's unseemly appearance.

Hickory was there to unhitch the buggy as soon as Emma turned into the yard.

"Thank you Hickory," Emma said as he helped her down. Iris sprang from her seat and was hurrying to the house when Emma called after her, "Iris, please walk! And don't forget to check on your father." She then added, "I think it best that we rest for a while before Mr. Hadley arrives."

Iris didn't feel like resting, but quickly decided not to object since she wanted to be alone. She had waited so long for this day to come and was determined not to let anything, or anyone, ruin it for her. "I'll be ready by then," she called over her shoulder.

Iris was surprised to see her father propped up in the bed when she entered his room. She hurried to sit down beside him, "Father, I'm glad that you're feeling better. Are you anxious to see the horses come in?"

"Yes," Edward replied, his voice somewhat stronger.

Iris clasped her hands under her chin. "You're doing so much better," she exclaimed. "Before you know it you'll be walking all over the house."

"And...and get...getting scolded," Edward smiled knowingly.

Iris laughed. "That reminds me, Aunt Emma wants me to rest before Mr. Hadley arrives."

"Hadley?" Edward's eyes filled with speculation.

"Remember, he's Mr. Harwick's assistant. He's coming for dinner, and then he's going to help Hickory carry you downstairs and into the wagon."

"I don't ne...need help dow...down the stai...stairs," Edward groaned defiantly.

Iris smiled, proud of her father's strong will. She patted his big hand draped across his knee. "That might be true, but you know how Aunt Emma worries. Besides, we don't want to take any chances. Someday I want you to paint a picture of the horses, and that will only happen if you get to go."

Edward didn't reply but seemed instead, to be considering the possibilities when Iris decided to tell him about Andrew's proposal. She couldn't keep it from him any longer.

"There's something I need to tell you Father. I...I hope you'll be happy for me." She couldn't help but notice a look of tender yearning in his eyes. He knows, she thought, he can tell that I'm in love. She continued, hopeful. "Andrew Burgess has asked me to marry him, and I said yes. I...I know that at first you didn't approve of him, but I'm certain it's because you don't know him the way I do." Iris studied the sudden disconcerted look on her father's face and her hopes began to wane. "Aunt Emma thinks I'm being impulsive, but I'm not. I love Andrew and he loves me."

"I...if only sh...she could be here," Edward muttered.

Iris grew concerned. Was he talking about her mother, and of the love they once shared? "I wish mother was here too," she said, hoping the words would be of some comfort to him. Instead he became agitated, his hands fidgeting across the bedspread as though he was searching for a small missing piece of a puzzle. Iris reached out and took his hand in hers. "I'm sorry if I've upset you Father, but I had to tell you. I couldn't keep it from you any longer. Andrew and I want you to be happy for us."

"Ivy is...is on the wall...there," Edward stammered, shakily pointing across the room.

Confused, Iris trembled, afraid that she had said too much. She leaned over and gently kissed her father's cheek. "The ivy's fine. It looks beautiful with the roses."

Tears welled in her father's eyes. Iris' lips pressed firmly together as she struggled to fight the painful lump in her throat. "I don't want you to worry Father. I'll always be here for you. I promise. Andrew plans to start a ranch. We're going to raise horses."

The room filled with a dreadful silence that made Iris want to jump up and run away. Instead, she forced herself to gain a measure of composure. She stood up, nodding reassuringly. "I'm going to rest now, and I want you to rest too. I'll be back." She turned at the door. "We can talk more later. For now, just think about the drive and how exciting it will be."

Edward fell back against the pillows. Iris watched for a moment as he lay quietly staring across the room at the picture of her mother. She gently closed the door, wondering what her father thought when he gazed at the captivating image on the wall.

...

Iris' mind was too full of conflicting thoughts and emotions for her to rest. Should she have waited to tell her father about Andrew's proposal? Was she wrong to have said 'yes' to Andrew without consulting her father first? To what lengths would Victoria Bishop go to try to steal Andrew away from her? Lying across the bed, wide awake, she clenched her fist. Why did her father keep talking about the ivy? Why did it bother him so?

She was anxious for Andrew's return. She needed to feel his arms around her, to hear him say that he loved her and that he still wanted to marry her. She closed her eyes, remembering the feel of his lips touching hers. Her insides warmed softly. She imagined his welcoming kiss, their faces hidden beneath the brim of his Stetson. A feeling of peaceful desire told her that she was right to have said 'yes' to him. She couldn't risk losing him.

Finding it impossible to still her disquieting thoughts, Iris got up and started to dress for dinner. She chose a simple pink sprigged poplin, and then took her time brushing her hair.

Later, Hickory carefully helped Edward down the stairs and into the dinning room. Everyone was happy to see Edward's rapid progress and a festive mood prevailed at supper. The drone of anxious talk filled the room. Though Mr. Hadley was as cordial a guest as any, he couldn't hide the fact that he was glad to be a part of the family adventure. He announced that Mr. Harwick was back in town and insisted on being called should the Bransons' return and cause further trouble. Mr. Hadley's face beamed heroically when Emma smiled, pleased with his news. They briefly shared in, what Aunt Emma referred to as, pleasant conversation. Mr. Hadley appeared mildly amused when Emma's face unexpectedly lit up as soon as supper was over and Iris announced that she was going to change and ride over to the ridge. Katie bustled about removing the dishes while Stella's cheerful banter could be heard from the kitchen every time Katie swung open the door.

Hickory helped Edward climb into the bed of the wagon, where Edward then positioned himself on a straight-back chair. The screen door clacked shut and Iris came bounding out of the house dressed in her violet-blue jersey riding habit with her hair braided to one side. Hickory had reined Honey in front of the house. As Iris quickly mounted she saw Mr. Hadley helping her aunt into the wagon where she sat down beside Edward. Iris flicked her gathered reins and Honey, eager to run, started off at a brisk canter. Iris shouted, "I'll meet you at the ridge," then galloped like the wind down the length of Stoney Creek Road.

It wasn't long before she reached the crest of the ridge. There was no rumbling sound of the horses in the wind that came in conflicting gusts. Iris held the reins tight in an effort to keep Honey stationed in one place while she eagerly scanned the view below. In the far distance she saw two people on horseback galloping fast across the open valley. She recognized one of the horses that Rebecca usually rode and, assuming that the other rider was Rebecca's brother, she decided they must be heading out to meet the herd. She stood in the stirrups and waved, calling excitedly, wishing desperately that she was down there with them instead of sitting idle. When there was no response she fell back in her saddle, wondering for a disappointed moment why Rebecca didn't tell her that she would be going with her brother instead of meeting her on the ridge. For now, there was little room in her mind for speculation. Every ounce of her being was filled with the sound of the meadowlarks that flitted above the flowering prairie grass. She peered longingly at the setting sun as it peaked the treetops, crowning every inch of the horizon in linked shades of muted ochres. The tree trunks remained a dark walnut color, a silhouette as Iris was, a charcoal sketch on the landscape.

Suddenly the breeze carried a sound like that of distant rumbling thunder. Amidst that tremulous roar Iris heard what sounded like a succession of rapid rifle shots. She recognized the forceful pounding pulse of the wild horses and the powerful call of the drover's whips as they led the stallions and trailing mares toward home. She flew around in her saddle, scanning the road behind her for any sign of her father. She saw the approaching wagon and motioned frantically for them to hurry.

"They're coming!" she shouted. "I can hear them." She swept around and bellowed, "Yee-haw!" caring little that she sounded like a field hand.

Momentarily the wagon pulled up beside Iris' horse. Hickory and Mr. Harwick jumped down and hurriedly carried Edward to the edge of the ridge.

...

In one fell swoop they came, filling the air with a sound like that of hollow thunder. The power of the enormous herd touched Iris' very being with a maddening ferocity. She stood in her stirrups, waving excitedly, hoping Andrew could see her amidst the billowing cloud of dust.

"Look father!" she cried. "They're wilder than the whole country." She turned to see her father's expression and there were tears in his eyes. Iris wasn't upset. She knew they were happy tears and she was thrilled. She looked back at the rumbling valley and was awe struck by the sight of the charging horses, their powerful bodies lunging forward, their muscled legs battering the earth while their manes recklessly cut into the wind.

Like her father, Iris loved everything there was to love about this country. She turned her face into the gusts sweeping up onto the ridge from the expanse below, touching everything in its path with the sweet scent of spring. Iris's heart reached out to the land with a love that was nearly as strong as her love for life itself. The thought brought warm tears to her eyes. Suddenly the herd turned with the out riders whose commanding calls and snapping whips echoed through the valley. When Iris realized that they were headed toward the dry river bed she shouted in a high, shrill voice, "They're turning toward the Stevens' place."

"It won't be long now," Hickory stated proudly, his shoulders squared, his hands tucked in his hip pockets.

Emma's eyes misted at the sight, her lips pursing tightly while Mr. Hadley, who had earlier removed his glasses, stared in speechless wonder.

"I...I never th...thought I would li...live to see it happen." Edward spoke above the deafening sound of the stampeding beasts that continued to cut a swath for miles, like the Red Sea, through the swaying grassland.

Mesmerized, no one responded. Iris thought of Andrew harnessing all that power and she was filled with a respect for him that she never knew was lacking until just then. He would build his ranch, and she would be there to share in his dream. She silently vowed to stick by his side, cheering him on, no matter what befell them over the years.

When the massive torrent started rounding a stand of cottonwood trees Iris swept up her reins and whipped Honey around. Seeing the contented look on her father's face she smiled. "Someday I want you to paint that father, exactly the way it is now." Her attention turned to her aunt who was talking excitedly with Mr. Hadley.

Eager to leave, Iris was painfully polite. "I'm sorry to

interrupt, but I have to go. I told Andrew that I'd meet him at the corral when he came in."

Emma smiled knowingly. "You'd better hurry on then. We'll see you back at the house.

Sensing an eagerness, Honey pranced nervously, tugging at the bit, ready to take on the wind. Iris patted the horse's strong lean neck.

Emma hurriedly added, "Make sure that he sees you Iris, no matter what."

Knowing that Victoria Bishop would be there, ready to vie for Andrew's attention, Iris whipped her reins around and jabbed Honey's flanks, spurring her into a swift gallop.

...

As she neared the Stevens' ranch, Iris could hear the horses hooves pounding the ground headed for the corral. She hauled back on her reins and, breathing heavily, she leaned over the pommel peering passed the trees where she saw an enormous wall of dust. The sound was deafening, almost frightening as it vibrated the ground for miles. Honey flinched and Iris reached out a comforting hand, smoothing her neck. She gently nudged Honey forward, realizing how close she really was when she caught a glimpse of the massive herd. Feeling the enormous affects of their breath taking power and knowing that only a few short weeks ago they had roamed wild, Iris suddenly grasped what harnessing them meant to Andrew. Alerted by her thoughts, she was afraid that she wouldn't make it to the Stevens' before Andrew reached the corral. Determined, she turned Honey to one side, prodding her anxiously into the ravine and up the opposite embankment to an abandoned road that she knew would take her to the ranch in a hurry.

Honey flew down the road as though drawn toward the wild herd. When Iris saw the grove of trees she wanted to slip through, she jerked back on the reins, coaxed Honey through the overhanging boughs, then sidled her down the bank into the gully and up onto the road. She quickly scanned the horizon behind her.

161

A short distance away she saw Andrew directing the lead stallion, who turned the herd toward the road in one fluid movement. For a swift moment the sight left Iris breathless. The deluge of teeming horse flesh continued to move as one, filled with an indescribable fervor, not yet aware that their journey was nearly over. The stallion was more beautiful than any animal Iris had ever seen. His black glistening chest was as wide as the length of Honey's mane while his long sinewy legs seemed on fire as they ripped the ground in front of him. Iris gasped. Anxious to get further ahead, she jabbed her heels against Honey's flanks and the horse sprang into a swift gallop, racing like lightening down the gravel road. A resulting surge like wildfire created adrenaline that whipped through Iris' body, causing a feeling of unstoppable exhilaration. It was happening! They would meet as planned. Andrew would see her waiting for him by the corral with an unmistakable look of love in her eyes. Her heart would crumble at the sight of his smile when he bent down to hand her the ribbon, just like he had promised he would.

Iris gripped the reins, turning Honey into the Stevens' yard when all at once her heart lurched. She jerked the reins so hard that Honey threw her head to one side and reared with a loud vexing snort. She pranced, her hooves snapping the ground repeatedly. Through white daggers that nearly blinded her vision, Iris glared at Victoria Bishop who was standing poised near the corral. She was dressed in what appeared to be a pristine cloud of billowing flowered batiste, her blonde hair swept up with a few dainty tendrils dripping down her swan's neck like droplets of honey.

Iris managed the reins while fighting for every irate breath that threatened to burst her lungs. Obtrusive thoughts careened through her mind like hail stones slamming into her heart. She knew what she had to do. Victoria needed to be put in her place. This was Nebraska where every man knew his territory and his boundary, not Boston where bids for property were placed in deceptive hearts over fine Dresden tea cups.

Her mind made up, Iris loosened her tethered grip and took a deep breath. Her only fear, which would make her appear weak, was that she would ride up to Victoria, see her coy smile and slap the practiced look of desire off her porcelain face. She jabbed her heels into Honey's sides and cantered toward the gate where Andrew had promised to meet her. She wasn't about to let him down. This was her deciding moment. She knew that Victoria would go to any length to try to win him over. Determined, Iris would be right behind her, no matter how far Victoria was prepared to go.

Iris stopped her horse in front of the sugar coated yards of peach colored flounces and quickly observed Victoria who was primping with the tips of her buffed fingernails. When Victoria looked up, Iris offered an amiable smile.

Victoria smiled gracefully in return. "I was wondering if you were going to show up," she said, unable to disguise the disappointment in her voice.

Iris ignored the quip. She dismounted and tethered her reins. She looked toward the house and saw Ida and a few of the house servants gathered on the porch. A few of the hired hands lingered near the hitching posts. One of the men was headed toward her, no doubt he felt obliged to take Honey over to the stable. Ida waved excitedly and Iris waved back. It was a thrilling moment for everyone. She thanked the hand and he nodded cordially. Then, Iris watched in amazement while the man, who resembled a bean pole, brushed down his dusty mustache, drew back his narrow shoulders, briefly swiped the dust from his tattered vest, and somehow remembered to tip his battered hat when he smiled clumsily at Victoria, all the while tripping over his crusty boots on his way to the stable. Why wasn't Victoria smiling sweetly back at him? After all he was a man, a cowboy.

Iris hid her smile then peered at the fading violet rays of dusk stretching across the windy prairie and was comforted. "Sounds like they're headed this way. It won't be long now," she stated matter of factly at Victoria who was re-positioning her fitted bodice.

Victoria's face lit up, her shoulders lifting slightly as she toyed with a loose strand of hair. "It's just like reading one of those romances, you know, with the wild horses and handsome daring cowboys and all."

Iris had never read a romance but was nonetheless convinced that Victoria would quickly change her mind when the onslaught of horses came storming toward the corral. She knew she should probably warn her, but concluded that experience was life's greatest teacher. Instead, she climbed on the rail fence, smiling down at Victoria as she did so.

Within minutes there was the sound of successive shrill whistles from the outriders, followed by snapping whips as the herd came clamoring into the expansive yard, stirring up a cloud of dust that blocked out what was left of the twilight sky. Iris immediately caught sight of Andrew. She thought how startling handsome he looked turned in his saddle with his back straight and his face partially concealed by the brim of his tipped Stetson. She waved her arms excitedly while watching in amazement as, at an easy canter, he and the drovers adeptly divided the herd, channeling the mares and fillies toward a nearby paddock, while somehow managing to marshal the rest of the horses into the corral. In her eagerness to see every move Andrew made Iris forgot to watch for Victoria's reaction. She was alerted when she heard a series of dry hacking coughs and looked down the length of the fence where she caught sight of the wilting pansy flapping a delicate white handkerchief in front of her puckered face. Victoria was squealing some inaudible complaint about her dress and the filthy smell that she would never be able to wash from her hair. When she started running toward the house, her arms flailing at her sides, Iris suppressed the desire to burst out into laughter by quickly turning away. That's when she saw Andrew riding toward her, his horse at an eager trot. Her hands came together, her face beaming, while the words she had practiced so well refused to form on her trembling lips.

"You made it!" she exclaimed. "I knew you would. I watched you from the ridge and you were magnificent!"

Andrew winked, his smile highlighting the ruddy glow on his cheeks. "I was that amazing, huh?"

"Every bit and more," Iris replied.

He quickly knotted his reins, swung a leg around the pommel then reached inside his shirt and withdrew Iris' blue hair ribbon. He leaned over and slid his gloved finger along her flushed cheek before he tied the ribbon to her braid, then touched the length to his lips. "I did it all for you Iris, if your answer is still yes."

Iris read the desire in Andrew's eyes like a poem that lacked a final confession. A cry escaped her parted lips and she sprang up and threw her arms around his neck. "Yes! yes! yes!" She leaned back slightly, their eyes meeting like magnets. "Is that convincing enough?" she queried, overcome by a look of gentle warmth on his face, "Or would a kiss convince you more?"

Andrew's eyes sparkled when he smiled. "I'm not a gambling man, so I'd better take what's offered to me."

He pulled her up into his arms where she was enveloped by the smell of leather and warm summer wind laced with the scent of spirited horses. When their lips met all was forgotten until they were jolted to reality by shrill whistles from the drovers, followed by the sound of clapping coming from the direction of the porch. Iris turned her head and saw Victoria, her pristine skirts wadded in her clenched fists as she stumbled up the coarse wood steps in a hurried effort to escape the settling dust. Iris smiled. The drive was over. Andrew was home safe. He had come back for her, like he had vowed he would.

CHAPTER TWENTY-THREE

Memories dancing down the hall
Hidden ivy on the wall

A hazy moon was just starting to rise, the evening breeze settling to a whisper when Iris dismounted in front of the stable. Hickory came out of the barn to retrieve Honey's reins.

"Your aunt just left with Ted. Mrs. Archer's fixin' to have her baby."

Iris took in a deep breath and hesitantly glanced back at the house. Reaching for the reins she said, "Maybe I should ride over there to see if they need any more help."

Hickory shook his head politely. "You might need to talk to Stella about leavin'. Before your aunt left, she mentioned something about you lookin' after your father. Seems he went and wore himself out with all today's excitement."

Iris' breath left her in a sigh. With her lips pressed tightly together she muttered, "I never thought about that." She paused for a moment then asked, "Did Aunt Emma send for the doctor?"

"I told her I'd run into town and get him but she didn't seem too worried. That's when Ted said the doc was already over at the Archer's. No doubt your aunt will ask him to stop by in the mornin'."

Relieved, Iris smiled in thought. "Father had a great time didn't he Hickory?"

"Sure thing. Nothin' short of a cyclone could of kept him from goin'."

"I'm so glad that he went. I think he'll recover quicker now that he's been out some."

Hickory nodded as he led Honey toward the stable. "Well, Stella's waitin'. I'm sure your aunt will send for you if they need any more help." He spoke confidently.

"Thanks Hickory." Iris started briskly toward the house then turned and called out. "Hickory, would you please brush

Honey down for me?"

"Consider it done," Hickory replied just before disappearing into the dark stable.

...

Edward lay in the fast growing darkness struggling with his thoughts and piqued emotions. He was tired of staying in bed like a helpless baby watching life go by through frilled curtains. There were so many things he needed to do, things that hadn't seemed urgent before his illness. He wanted to finish painting the windmill, and the horses...he had to do a painting of the horses. He grimaced. His eyes closed, he turned his head and stared at the blank wall. Maybe he shouldn't have gone to the ridge. It brought back so many unsettling memories of when he and Lydia were young. She was so beautiful then. How could he ever forget those inviting blue eyes and fanning black lashes set above her creamy pink cheeks, causing her to look like a blossoming pansy ready to be picked?

Edward winced at the thought of loosing her. He had thought she loved Nebraska the way that he did; but he was wrong. It didn't take him long to discover his mistake in bringing her out here. But what else could he have done? He had a farm that he had already put a lot of money into. He couldn't just leave it all behind and go back east, where Lydia wouldn't be happy until he was a dandy, flaunting himself amidst Boston's elite.

Edward slowly sat up with his feet on the floor. He looked at the window where a gentle breeze pushed its way across the prairie and into the room. It felt good, like a soft hand stroking his worn body. Twilight had settled and the gibbous moon was just beginning to rise in the distance where the outbuildings loomed like remnants of passing clouds. He bent over with his head in his spread hands. Dark thoughts entered his mind uninvited then searched through his tired body before resting heavily against his breast. His mind whispered of the past, "It was during the night. That's what the sky looked like when she left." His breathing accelerated and he clutched the sheets. He fought to calm himself, his eyes closed tightly in an effort to blot out the truth. Would the demons ever stop haunting him? Would the pain never cease? How could he forget her when every time he looked at Iris he was reminded of the only woman he had ever loved? What had Lydia done to him all those years ago that caused him to crumble at the mere thought of her? He tried so many times to find someone else to fill the void in his heart, but there had never been another woman compared to Lydia. Was it a curse? Was he destined to die alone? Had that been God's plan all along? He shook his head violently to rid himself of the burning anguish. "No!" he wailed. He was always forced to admit that it was him, not her, or God. He was the one that first spoke of love. He was the one that made the prairie appear as inviting as a tender kiss. He still loved her, but she was gone. The only thing left was his wretched deceit.

"Father? Are you all right?"

Edward started then turned and saw Iris standing on the other side of the bed. His lashes batted away the ghostly images and he nodded a quick reply.

"Were you calling me?" she asked quietly.

He was disturbed by the worried look on his daughter's face. Apprehension gripped him like a vise. What strength he had left quickly drained from his body, leaving him feeling defeated. He peered intently at her, the exact image of Lydia, and then hurriedly looked away. She knew. She was beginning to suspect that she had been lied to all these years. If only he knew how to reassure her, to tell her that it was a necessary lie and not one meant to harm her. If only he could say what needed to be said. He couldn't tell her now, not when he recalled how happy she looked on the ridge waiting for Andrew to come back to her. If only he had told her sooner. His mind whirled, his pulse quickened with fear and regret. He could feel his face beading with sweat. His breath caught as he fought to calm himself. "I...I was..ju...just try...ing to...to move around...a little."

Iris hurried to his side. "Here, let me help you," she offered, touching his shoulder caringly.

Edward shook his head. "I...I'm...ti...tired now. I th...think I'...ll just go to b...bed."

"Are you going to be all right, Father? You look a little pale."

Edward quickly shook his head. If he spoke now, then maybe the evil memories would go away and leave him in peace. She had to know before it was too late. "I...I wan...ted to tell..you a...bo...ut ivy...over there...on the wall." He raised his eyes.

Iris smiled lovingly. "Don't worry about that now, Father. You need to rest."

Out of breath, Edward fell heavily against the pillows and closed his eyes. Iris stroked his damp forehead then drew a coverlet over him. She waited until he was breathing calmly before she kissed him and left the room. He slowly raised his eyelids when he heard the door click shut. Bitter tears trickled down his cheeks forming a warm pool in his sideburns. For once he didn't bother to wipe them away. He listened to the sounds of the night just outside the window and thought of all the times he had laid beside Lydia. Now he lay awake fighting the urge to cry, afraid to face the truth. All at once the tears poured from his eyes and his chest heaved as great racking sobs spilled onto his pillow. The time had come. He would free himself of the miserable secret. Iris would finally know the truth. He tried to move, but he was so tired. He called for her, and then waited for the sound of her footsteps. He waited in silence; his eyes grew heavy, his very being weary from sobbing. His web-like thoughts began to fade as his body was slowly shrouded in sleep.

...

Iris woke early the next morning; and, casting aside the thought of wearing a corset and a clumsy petticoat, she quickly pulled on her britches and the delft blue work shirt her aunt despised seeing her wear. She rapidly brushed her hair and in her haste only braided it half way down her back before she secured it. She would grab something quick to eat, just to please Stella, and then hurry over to Rebecca's to see the baby. She looked out the window and noticed a dark bank of clouds gathering in the west. She mentally shrugged off the thought of rain. By the time the storm arrived she would be back home. As she belted her blouse she made a mental note to ask Rebecca if she could ride over to the Stevens' with her to watch the men work with the horses. Rebecca would go if she thought Todd would be there.

...

Iris scurried down the hall, stopping only momentarily to listen at her father's door. There was no sound. It was early; no doubt he was still sleeping soundly after all the excitement yesterday.

She fluttered down the stairs and was headed toward the kitchen when she heard Stella talking excitedly. The urgency in her voice made Iris halt. She backed away until she was slightly hidden by the wall near the entry to the kitchen.

"Dis is all wrong," Stella said, fighting to keep her voice down. "Da two of dem leaving like dat, vit out telling anyvone vhere day vere going."

Iris pressed her head against the wall, her eyes raised in thought.

"First Miss Bishop leaves then Todd and Rebecca run away," Katie stated reflectively.

Iris's mind whirled for a quick moment. Victoria left? Rebecca gone? Her thoughts were jarred by Stella's quick response.

"Vit vhat I've heard about dat voman da train didn't leef fast enough to suit me."

"Are you sure she left?" Katie inquired.

The sound of clattering dishes disrupted Stella's answer.

"...home til five dis morning. One of da hands from the Stevens' place was drivin' Miss Bishop to town to catch da train vhen dey saw da Archer's vagon and stopped to ask about da baby. Dat's vhen Miss Stratton found out dat da flousy was leavin' town."

Iris heard Katie's light footsteps cross the room before

there was the sound of flatware clanging. "Did Miss Stratton tell him about the baby?"

Iris's back stiffened as a sudden feeling of ill will engulfed her.

"I didn't haf da heart to ask," Stella spoke in a heavy voice. It mat me hav a painful memory. I can't bear to tink of it happening again."

Iris couldn't take the suspense any longer. The voices in the kitchen stopped abruptly at the sound of her shoes rapidly tapping the flagstones. She flew into the kitchen like a bird caught in unfamiliar surroundings. When she saw the looks on Stella's and Katie's faces she knew that something was dreadfully wrong.

"What's happened?" her voice trembled.

Stella's hands clasped tightly under her ample bosom, her face white with uncertainty, while Katie's large eyes remained blank.

"Where's Aunt Emma?" Iris insisted sharply.

"She's asleep," Stella offered awkardly.

"Then tell me what's wrong."

"Miss Bishop's left town," Katie was quick to answer. "Seems she's had her fill of livin'..."

"I don't care about her!" Iris scolded staunchly. "Where's Todd and Rebecca? And what's happened to Mrs. Archer's baby?"

There was a long pause before Stella hesitantly offered a reply. "It's not someting a lady chould hear."

"If you won't tell me, then I'll have to wake up Aunt Emma." Iris turned sharply and Stella scampered across the room to stop her.

"No! You'f forced me to tell you. Now I vill be da vone to haf to repeat da dreadful story."

Iris remained irate. "You didn't mind repeating it to Katie."

"Menschens kind!" Stella threw up her hands. "I vill haf to answer to your aunt vonce I tell you."

"No you won't," Iris roughly insisted, looking the cook squarely in the eye. "Now tell me, did the baby die?"

A bleak cry fell from Stella's pinched lips. Her eyes batted and she encircled them with her pursed fingertips. "Vone of dem did. Da odder vone is still alive."

"You didn't tell me that," Katie said breathless.

"She had twins?" The words caught in Iris's throat.

"I don't haf to tell you everyting!" Stella reprimanded Katie with a stern glare.

"Stop that! Tell me about Rebecca?" Iris implored.

Katie's eyes riveted on Stella whose expression was like that of a barn owl's. She replied morosely, "Her faddur has been searching all day for her and dat boy, and dey are novhere to be found."

Iris caught a sob, afraid that if she started to cry she wouldn't be able to stop. She recalled her brief conversation with Ida who was ladling up water for the men. It was after the drive, just before Iris left to go home. Ida had said that Todd's brother was there looking for Todd and Rebecca and that he'd just left. Iris quickly considered the situation when suddenly she remembered Ida having said that Todd never showed up for the drive. That's when Iris remembered seeing the two horses galloping across the valley. She now knew that it was Todd and Rebecca running away. Iris wondered why their running away would upset Stella so much. She looked at Stella, her eyes narrowing in thought.

"What did you mean when you said it...it was happening all over again?" she goaded.

Stella's hands flew to her face. "Aw! Don't ask me about dat! It was nutting."

Iris quickly looked at Katie who was gaping at Stella in disbelief. Avoiding her, Stella turned toward the table and shakily began cracking eggs into a bowl.

Incensed, Iris commanded, "Stop treating me like a child and answer me now!"

An egg slipped to the floor and Stella immediately began

to weep while Katie fled from the room like a frightened mouse.

Iris shouted, "Katie! Come back here right now or you'll be dismissed!"

Katie instantly appeared in the doorway, her face pinched and red as a beet. "I don't know anything, I promise. I was..."

Suddenly, from upstairs there was a loud resounding thump followed by a series of tumbling clatters that ended with the sound of shattering glass.

Iris let out a fearful cry and darted out of the room. Gripping the banister, she flung herself up the stairs to the landing where she met her aunt rushing from her room hastily tying on her wrap. They ran to Edward's room expecting to find him sprawled out on the floor, but instead he was sitting slumped over on the bed. Across the room the picture of Lydia was lying in a shattered heap on the floor amongst what was left of Edward's porcelain coffee mug.

Seeing that her father was all right Iris asked. "What happened?" as she hurriedly began picking up the pieces of broken glass.

Pointing a shaky finger at the wall, Edward replied soberly, "There's the truth."

Emma drew a sharp breath. "Edward," she said in a low frantic gasp.

Iris turned around and saw her aunt gripping her wrap tightly to her neck. Her face was as white as her taut knuckles. "What's wrong?" Iris urged.

Her aunt's eyes remained fixed on the disjointed pieces of bubble glass lying on top of the crumpled portrait. Iris looked back at the likeness of her mother, and then continued picking up the remnants, when suddenly light swatches of color appeared behind the torn canvas. Her hands began to shake as she felt herself weaken. She set aside the last piece of glass along with a ripped corner of the picture and her heart sank into despair when she saw an oil painting of two identical babies, their names, Iris and Ivy scrawled beneath tiny feet that peeked out from under matching gowns.

Dazed, Iris turned her head, feeling all the while like she was an abstract figure in a hazy dream. Her father's glazed eyes seemed to be looking through her, while the muscles in his jaw tightened. Her aunt looked like a fearful ghost trapped in someone's wispy memory. No one moved. No one spoke. Iris could tell by the distant look on their faces that they had, at some moment, mentally left the events taking place in the room, and were now coming back from the past.

CHAPTER TWENTY-FOUR

Weeping willow all alone
In a wide and open meadow
No one's ever coming home
How long the evening shadows

Iris appeared outwardly unfazed by the revelation, while deep inside her mind wrestled with the thought of hidden deceit. The clarity that had left her was slowly easing it's way back into her body, bringing with it a quaking she was unable to control. She felt the tremor and with it came a slow dissolving of the long nurtured feeling of trust. Her eyes remained riveted on her aunt who appeared stunned. Willing herself to remain calm, Iris found her voice that sounded strained and unnatural.

"What is this?"

Emma tensed, her hands laced tightly to the pit of her stomach. Her lips parted but there were no words, only a quick succession of short, raspy breaths. Her spread fingers shakily flew to her head that was flinching from side to side.

Iris' mind spun around the intended distraction. Her body was beginning to quaver. "Answer me!" she pleaded, her voice convulsing.

Alarmed, Emma covered her mouth to stay her cry. Her forlorn eyes reddened, filling with tears. She hastily wrested her wrap tightly around her body. Gathering a long breath she tried to speak but only managed to stammer an unintelligible reply.

Edward gruffly interrupted her fearful spasm, admitting in a broken voice. "It means... th...that I've been liv...ing a lie that has...has now ended."

The dismal confession echoed through Iris' head like the sound of air traveling through a vent. The thudding in her heart plummeted deep into her bowels, leaving her feeling breathless, her insides churning. Afraid of what her father was going to say next, afraid that she was going to be sick; she covered her ears and fled from the room leaving behind the muffled sound of hurried footsteps and frantic voices.

Iris ran down the hall, flew open the attic door and clambered noisily up the narrow stairwell. Stepping clumsily onto the dusty flooring she peered at the cramped space that was full of shadows created by the half light slanting through the rectangular window. The wind brushed against the pane and in the distance thunder crackled, reminding her that a storm was approaching. Suddenly afraid of finding what she had come for, she covered the lower half of her face with stiffened fingertips and closed her eyes tight, afraid that any moment she would start crying and never stop.

It was only a short while ago that she had envisioned the attic as being a place of enchantment, a place where wistful dreams were weaved. Now this dark webbed room was nothing but a tomb besmeared with lies and treacherous secrets. She caught a painful sob, her insides coiling in an effort to keep it down. She needed to be with Andrew, to feel his arms around her, to be told that she was loved and that he would never leave her.

Shoving back the burning pain lunging in her throat, Iris began rummaging through old kitchen tins, piles of books and cast aside hat boxes, pillows started in needlepoint and never finished, wrapped in worn pillow slips and banished to a place amongst the creaky rafters beside a frayed straw hat and a bundle of tied fishing poles. Then she remembered where she had seen what she had thought were quilt remnants and she hurriedly moved across the floor boards to a small table stacked with old books. When she spotted the familiar material she jerked up the burgundy plaid taffeta and tears gushed from her eyes. She wiped them with the back of her hand but couldn't keep herself from crying. She batted her weighted lashes, gazing through a blurred veil. She smoothed down the small skirt that hid a little eyelet petticoat and bloomers, and a black pair of dainty strapped leather boots, revealing the figure of a porcelain doll with looped ebony curls painted around her heart shaped face. The doll had current eyes with long spidery lashes and red lips the color and size of wild strawberries. The hovel-like room darkened for a moment when a cloud passed swiftly over the sun before the pale light returned. Iris looked at the cradle hunkering in the shadows nearby and she saw the 'I' carved on the back and instantly knew that it was Ivy's. She remembered having asked about the cradle on the day of the picnic. Aunt Emma had said then that there was another baby, a baby that had died. Iris swallowed hard. With her eyes pursed and her jaws clamped she silently vowed never to ask if there had in fact been another baby. She didn't want to know the truth.

Clutching the doll to her chest she shuddered then turned and scrambled down the steep steps and fled down the hall to her room. She slammed the door then hastily began rummaging through her trunk, tossing its contents on the floor beside her until she found what she was looking for. She shakily reached into the flowery cavern and pulled out a doll identical to the one caught under her arm. Nausea rolled at the back of her throat as she brought the two dolls together. She knew there was more that had been left unsaid, but she was too terrified to think about it. "Why?" she cried. Possible alibis kept assailing her mind when a thought suddenly struck her. Could it be true? She sprang toward the door. Could her mother still be alive?

...

Iris approached her father's doorway just as her aunt was moving swiftly across the room to the armoire where he was struggling to pull a valise from the overhead shelf. Dr Sheldon, who had arrived while Iris was in the attic, moved quickly to help him but Edward adamantly flung his arm back.

Visibly shaken, Emma pleaded, "Edward, what are you doing?"

"I'm go...ing to Boston," he answered firmly. Fighting to subdue his emotions he continued. "I'm go...going to find Lydia."

"You can't do that!" Emma reprimanded stoutly. "You're in no condition to go anywhere."

Dr. Sheldon stood uncomfortably at the foot of the bed. "Edward, she's right. That may not be a wise decision with..."

Iris' father jerked his head around, the burrows on his forehead deepening. "I'll go if I...I damn well pl..ease," he shouted. "And no...no one, or noth...ing will stop me this time. Do...do you hear me? No one!"

Then it was true!

A cry escaped Iris' lips while a rippling chill gripped her spine. Sweeping into the room, angry tears glimmering in her eyes, she thrust out the identical dolls and in a forced, conclusive tone she demanded, "She didn't die did she?"

Startled, her father whirled around, nearly falling over backwards. When he saw the dolls clutched in Iris' angry grip his shoulders shrunk and he dropped the valise at his feet. Iris could see instantly, by the stricken look on his face that he was dredging up painful memories and, despite the hurt inside of her, she felt sorry for him.

"No," he answered morosely. She left...just af...ter you were born with...with Ivy...your...your sis...ter."

Aghast, Emma cried, "Edward wait! Please."

Breathless, Edward lowered his head. "I'm tired of...of waiting. All it...it's brought me is mis...misery and pain."

Still reeling from an onslaught of unanswered questions, Iris fought back the agony that was fast rising inside of her. She leered at her aunt who stood motionless. "You knew all along and you didn't say anything," she accused stiffly.

Tears sprouted on Emma's lashes. "I told you. It...it wasn't for me to say. You...you have to understand..."

"No!" Iris cried defiantly. "I don't! Don't ask me to understand, or to forgive, or...or anything! I don't owe any of you anything!"

Her eyes livid, she threw the dolls on the bed glaring intently at her father. "You told me that she died. All this time I felt sorry for you because I thought she died giving birth to me." An estranged cry slipped from her parted lips. "How could you...

you lie to me like that?"

Tears rolled down Edward's face and Emma dropped her head in her open hands and began sobbing quietly. Edward's shoulders hugged his neck like a scarf, his head shaking while his stark eyes remained transfixed. "It...it...was too pain...ful to even admit to my...self." his voice staggered.

"All these years!" Iris lamented. She started to run from the room when she ran into Stella who had slipped up the stairs and was standing like a lumbering shadow in the hallway just outside the door. She put out her hand to keep Iris from escaping.

"Don't blame your faddur for vhat's happened, Iris. You chood blame me. I knew da whole story and I vas wrong not to say someting."

"Why should you have said anything?" Iris assailed. "When no one else saw the need to tell me the truth?"

"Because dere are parts of da story day don't know." Stella extended her hand and in it Iris saw a battered book. "Dis belongs to you," Stella said. She glanced at the look of disbelief on Emma's face and sighed regretfully, "No one efer tolt you dat da girl who nursed Iris after her muddur left vas...vas my daughter." There was a moment of muddled silence where it appeared that Stella was sorting through her thoughts.

Shocked, Emma looked at Edward who appeared stunned.

Stella went on,"Vhen your muddur vas wid child she discovered dat da girl doing da laudry vonce a veek coot hand stitch and embroider, and so she hired her to...to sew her baby tings."

"You told Mrs. Stratton that your daughter could do fancy work?" Emma stared in disbelief.

Without raising her head Stella replied. "I...I vanted her to haff a better position so I...yes...I tolt her dat...but..." she hastened, her eyes slightly raised, "It vas da trut, I taught her myself." She waited to see if there would be a reprimand and when there was none she continued. "Da only ting I didn't tell her vas dat Livvy had a baby." Her eyes narrowed, "It vas dat goot fur nutting stable boy dat caught her eye."

Tears sprouted on Stella's lashes and Iris winced, suddenly feeling like she was caught in a horrifying nightmare. Before she could even think of what to say or do next Stella continued, "She barely finished making da little clothes vhen...vhen..."

Stella looked cautiously across the room at Edward and Iris realized how afraid she was, but she didn't understand why. Her father had never been a mean man. All at once Iris thought of the truth that he had kept hidden from her all these years and she grimaced, her open palm pressed tightly against her churning stomach. She had likewise, never imagined her father to be a man who would purposely lie to her, or to anyone. Her disquieting thoughts were interrupted when Stella concluded, "...Vhen you and your sister vere born. It vas a short time after dat dat Livvy's baby died and...and den...den dat's vhen I tolt...," she glanced quickly at Emma, "Mr. Stratton dat I knew ov somvun who could nurse Iris, since she vas so sickly." Her words hastened. "Livvy...she vas da only vun who coot do it... vid her having lost her baby so suddenly and all." Her eyes grew heavy. "Later, vhen she died ov da milk fever I found out dat dis...," Stella looked at the diary in her hand, "vas to be buried wid her. It was thought that if the record of her past was buried wid her den maybe her sin vould be forgotten. Vhen I saw it beside her body in da casket I...I took it." Her head dropped and she cried openly. "I vouldn't...haf done... it, but Got...knows it vas all I hat...left of her."

A painful sob caught in Iris' throat as she reached out and took the book. She could hear the muffled sounds of her aunt crying and her father's erratic breathing as he struggled to compose himself, but none of that seemed to matter.

All she could think of was that her mother ran away and left her.

She was filled with an uncontainable feeling of dread. Its long dark, ghostly hand was reaching down into her very being, its gnarly fingers clutching at her heart, wringing what was left of her will from it. Stella was saying something, her weakened voice penetrated Iris' dulled senses.

"If you follow da...da rutted road just passed da old...da old Miller place..." she stammered."You'll come to a small unkempt apple orchart. Take da foot pat tru it...it's hard to follow because I'm da only vun who goes dere now. Pretty soon you'll come to a lichgate."

She seemed to be studying her hands folded against her body. "You don't know dis, but da old German church used to stand dere. It burnt down before you vere born. Some tought Got vas gone from dere after dat." She nodded reassuringly. "Dat's vhy she was allowed to be buried dere.

"Go tru it and you'll see a head stone beside a tumbled down vall wid lichen and moss and some vild ivy growing on it. Dat's vere Livvy is buried."

"Her name was Livvy?" Iris asked in a strained voice. "She took care of me after...after my mother left?"

"Vhen she vas born her faddur called her Lavina. It vas da name of a girl he vonce loffed back in Germany." Stella choked back a tremulous sob that seared Iris' heart then added, "I vas angry at first...dat he vould tink of his first loff vhen I just gaf him a daughter, but my baby vas so beautiful dat I couldn't stay mat for long."

"But why? Why did my mother leave me?" The parched words stumbled from Iris' lips in spurts like the disjointed pieces of glass still lying on the floor.

Stella looked up and for the first time since she had entered the room their eyes met, both filled with want. "It's all in dere, in da book," she said in a low voice.

Iris' face was void of all expression belying the turmoil that was raging inside of her. Was the whole world filled with such misery? She wanted to run, to get as far away from all of the eyes that were staring at her, the faces that were pleading for understanding and acceptance when there was none. She clutched the book to her chest and darted out of the room and down the

Debra L. Hall

steps. The front door slammed behind her and she ran toward the stable where she dragged open the door with more strength than she realized she had left in her. She ran to Honey and, quickly slipping a bridle over the horse's head, Iris gripped the reins along with the horse's long mane, then flung herself on to the horse's sturdy back, the way she had always wanted to but was taught was against propriety for any young lady who cared about her future and her family name.

CHAPTER TWENTY-FIVE

Katie was in the kitchen gathering scraps for the chickens when there was a knock at the front door. Dragging her wet hands down the front of her stained apron she grimaced. She grumbled, "Why do I always have to answer the door? Why can't they just hire a butler?" She hurried to the back door and pushing it open wide, she searched the yard for Stella. After having come down the stairs, Stella had gone to gather eggs, a job she insisted was Katie's, like answering the front door, and she was taking her time about coming back. Katie let the screen door slam shut. Setting aside the scrap bucket, she grumbled expecting to be scolded for dallying as she hurried down the hall. Pausing at the foot of the steps just in front of the door, she looked toward the landing where she could hear strained voices. The knock sounded again and she was quick to open the door.

Mr. Hadley was standing in the shade of the morning glories that wound their way up the trellis to the side of the porch. His back as straight as a broom stick; he was holding a small basket in his hand.

"Is Miss Stratton home?" he asked cordially.

Katie paused, unsure of what to say after the morning's untimely incident. "Umm," she nodded, glancing over her shoulder toward the dim staircase.

Mr. Hadley cleared his throat and Katie skittishly replied, "Come...come in Mr. Hadley." She moved to one side. "I'll...I'll tell Miss Stratton that you're here."

"Thank you, I'll just wait here. Please tell her that I have news of the utmost importance."

Katie nodded as rapidly as a lid bobbing on a hot tea kettle, and then swiftly ran up the steps.

"I can't go down looking like this!" Emma cried when Katie told her that Mr. Hadley was waiting for her on the front porch. Twisting the front of her wrap close to her chin she quizzed, "Did you ask him to come in?"

"Yes ma'am, but he wanted to stay outside. He said he has news of utmost importance. It's urgent," Katie reiterated in a voice that sounded as sophisticated as Mr. Hadley's.

"OHHH!" Emma rattled, "This is unthinkable." She glanced at Dr. Sheldon who was standing beside Edward's bed. In a calm voice he was speaking consolingly to Edward who was lying down.

With her hand spanning the full length of her loosely braided hair, Emma straightened her back primly and started down the steps in as lady-like a manner as possible, considering she would be facing the only man who had ever made her blush. As soon as she opened the door and stepped out onto the porch Brenton Hadley started at the sight of her in her night clothes. He quickly gathered his senses and doffed his hat, remembering to smile, and then looked away, as any gentleman would under the circumstance.

Emma quickly scanned the yard for any sign of Hickory, or any of the other hands. She would be mortified if they happened to see her standing on the front porch, of all places, talking to a man from town, especially with her being inappropriately dressed.

"Uhh, I...uhh, it appears that I've come at a bad time," Brenton said, awkwardly fumbling with his hat that was balancing on top of the basket.

Holding her wrap tightly to her body, without realizing that in doing so she accentuated her curved figure, Emma said, "I'm sorry, Mr. Hadley, but we've had some rather unsettling events take place this morning and I...well, I just haven't had a chance to get dressed."

Brenton was trying hard not to gawk. "I hope it's not Mr. Stratton. He's all right isn't he?"

For an awkward moment their eyes met and Emma's hand secured the printed folds of her wrap. "No...no, it's nothing like that," she said looking down. "I mean he's doing much better, thank you."

"No doubt the drive he took yesterday helped," Brenton stated before adding, "Is there anything I can do to be of assistance?"

Emma blinked back the tears that were threatening to fall and answered in a thin voice. "I'm afraid not...not yet anyway."

There was a moment of uncomfortable silence when neither one knew what to say and yet wanted painfully to say so much. Brenton cleared his throat nervously then remembered the basket and handed it to her shyly, "This is for you."

Emma responded with a smile, blushing clear down to her neck that was openly exposed when she reached her hand out. She lifted the lid and it creaked, followed by her tiny gasp of surprise. Her fingers were visibly shaking when she touched the black and white kitten that had quickly popped it's head up.

"A kitten! Oh, look at you, you're precious," Emma whispered softly against the kitten who wasted no time climbing into her open hand.

Feeling self-conscious, Brenton smiled with his lips pressed firmly together. "She's a little feisty. I thought you might like to call her Pepper."

"Pepper?" Emma giggled, nuzzling the cat. "If you think that suits her then Pepper it'll be." Emma smiled up at Brenton, forgetting for a moment that she was half dressed with her sunlit hair trailing over her breast. "You didn't come all this way just to bring me a kitten, did you Mr. Hadley?" She asked.

"Well, no. I...uh, as a matter of fact Mr. Harwick insisted I come right away as he's received news that the Bransons' are back."

Emma gasped, her eyes widening and Brenton spontaneously reached out and placed a comforting hand on her forearm. "Please don't be alarmed. They're being watched carefully. If you have the least bit of trouble, Mr. Harwick has given his assurance that they'll be arrested immediately." Brenton paused, and then nodded quickly. "If you need my protection, I'm willing to stay here until you feel safe. I...I can sleep in the barn or..."

Emma suppressed a smile. "That won't be necessary Mr. Hadley, Hickory's here and..."

"Please feel free to call me Brenton," he encouraged, his eyes fixed firmly on hers.

Emma felt certain that her face was redder than Stella's strawberry jam. The thought of Stella reminded Emma that she hadn't seen her for quite some time. Her head flew up and her heart quickened. Stella would be the last person she would want to find her flirting with Mr. Hadley, her mind corrected her, Brenton. There, lumbering slowly across the barn yard was Stella sheltering an apron full of eggs. Emma snatched her arm away from Brenton's lingering touch, their eyes meeting like two star-struck lovers and resuming her parlor manners, she spoke in a practiced voice.

"Thank you for coming Mr. Had...Brenton. And thank you for Pepper. It was so kind of you to think of me."

Brenton desperately wanted to tell her that he thought of her every moment of every day, but that wasn't why he had come. Instead, he continued twirling his hat between his thumb and forefinger while calmly relating the rest of Mr. Harwick's message.

"There is one more thing," he began before Emma's neck stiffened and her eyes strayed off in the direction where Stella was stooping near the lilac bush. With his head remaining still, his eyes shifted before they fixed back on Emma. "Mr. Harwick asked me to inform you that he has received a telegram from a woman named Lydia."

Emma's head whipped around. "Lydia!" she blurted.

Brenton nodded cordially. "That's all he said, Lydia. The telegram states that she will be in town soon and would like to meet with Mr. Stratton, after which she would like to be properly introduced to her Iris."

The color drained instantly from Emma's face while a series of shrill cries rattled from her parted lips. One hand flew to her throat, the other to her forehead as her head began to sway. Before Brenton could discern what was happening, Emma swooned and fainted in a crumpled heap amongst the shadows flickering through the flowering vines.

CHAPTER TWENTY-SIX

The wind blew them across the prairie
their hearts
their dreams
their very souls

Honey bolted down the length of Stoney Creek Road. It would eventually lead Iris to the old Miller place, and to the seldom used back road that would direct her to the abandoned cemetery. While growing up, she remembered hearing people talk about the old burial plot, mostly kids conjuring up ghost stories. Now it was a place that would tell her the truth about her past, the horrid truth that kept drumming in her head, echoing like the sound Rebecca's little brother made when he sat on the floor banging on a pot with a wooden spoon.

"Oh! Rebecca!" her mind cried. "Why didn't you tell me?" A new reservoir of tears filled Iris' eyes and she fell heavily into Honey's neck, comforted momentarily by her sure-footedness. Iris wondered how she could find out about Rebecca and Todd. There was no time to go to the Archers'. Her head thumped painfully. She needed to be alone. There was too much to think about, too much to contend with.

Thunder groaned slowly above her and she raised her eyes, watching the wind as it shifted the clouds, gathering them into dark huddles. A sudden feeling of desperation flared inside of her. She jabbed Honey's flanks, driving her to run as fast as she could so they could flee far away from the immense lie that was her past.

After galloping a short distance, Iris jerked back on the reins, swung her leg over Honey's neck and dropped to the ground. Thunder crackled overhead and she glanced up at the low hanging clouds, anxious to complete her mission. Spotting the old rutted road that Stella had mentioned, Iris wrapped the reins around a shrub and rushed toward a long row of cottonwood trees. Peering down the road ahead, she could see the old Miller place. Realizing that she was on the right road, she hurried along the crest of the bank and through the low hanging boughs. Hugging the diary close to her body, she prodded on, searching for signs that would tell her the apple orchard was near. When she spotted the small grove, the trees crowded together, like companions sharing a secret, her heart quickened, reminding her of the fearful truth that lay buried in the abandoned cemetery.

Before she was close enough to smell the tartness of apples wrapped in wavering leaves she saw the scanty opening that would take her to the footpath. She approached the hollow with some trepidation and carefully parted the bowed limbs. Once inside the depression, her steps hastened as it was darker inside the orchard than on the road. An ominous feeling surrounded her, causing her to shiver. Her mind raced fearfully, full of tales of ghosts and body snatchers. She scolded herself for acting like a scared child, then was momentarily comforted by the fact that it was only the heavy clouds that made the place seem so dark and terrible.

Suddenly her heart lurched. There, just ahead, she could see the lich gate bidding her to enter the cemetery. Feeling like a forbidden guest she stepped lightly on the soft, grassy earth overgrown with tiny wild flowers and wisps of creeping ground cover. Finally she reached the tumbled headstone. Hesitating, she dragged her hand from her faint heart and laid it on the cracked arch. She knelt down. Through a veil of warm tears she traced the chiseled letters smothered in cool green moss. She sat on the bedded undergrowth composed of years of fallen leaves and closed her eyes briefly. A cool breeze rustled the tree tops, sprinkling bits of light onto the open book in her lap. She touched the dried rose petals pressed between the pages while her eyes followed the delicately written words.

"The following true story was related to me in the year 1852 by my mistress, Lydia Stratton, a woman from Boston, and written by me, Lavina Getman at her request. It should be given to

Iris Stratton upon her eighteenth birthday. Should either one of us die before then, Mrs. Stratton request that the diary be buried with me for fear it will fall into the wrong hands.

"After receiving a large portion of his inheritance at age twenty-one, Edward Stratton left his home in Boston in search of wide-open places, finally settling for the wind blown grasslands of Nebraska. For many years he struggled to cultivate the abandoned homesteads he had purchased and before long he was landlord over five tenant farms that spanned westward from the Missouri river, lush farmland that produced the country's finest corn and wheat. He ran a large herd of cattle, owning enough dairy cows and hogs to provide sufficiently for himself and his tenants.

"Having captured the beauty of the prairie in water colors, Edward hung his paintings in the two-story Victorian house that he built in remembrance of his mother, who died a year after he left home.

"When Edward was thirty years old he was summoned to his father's death bed. Thereafter, while settling his father's estate, he met Lydia Rutledge, a twenty year old debutante. Lydia's parents strongly disapproved of their attachment. Edward was a farmer, a lifestyle, that her parents decided was unfit for a lady. Lydia refused to give him up. Edward was cordial and very sensitive to her needs; but her parents still threatened to send her away if she persisted. As a result, the young couple fled Boston, secretly marrying in a small township before heading to Nebraska and the house with the wrap around porch shaded by a rose laden trellis and jutting gables. Imagining rooms full of children, Lydia closed her eyes to the vast empty prairie, casting aside any wisp of regret.

"The house lay quiet for years, lacking the sound of a baby's cry or the comforting creak of a rocker. Instead, Lydia sat motionless near the window where she gazed empty-eyed at the vast windy prairie.

"How often she dreamed longingly of the life she had left behind. How could she ever forget the luncheons where ladies wearing multicolored silks and satins fluttered their lace fans over her mother's Dresden china which hosted delicate pastries, delivered from the most reputable bakery in town? Many a gentleman had wooed her, seeking her favors, or a simple dance at her first cotillion; after which she would stroll with the young man of her choice through the heavily scented rose garden where she had been kissed more than once.

"Suddenly a whirl of dusty leaves would dash against the lonely, rambling house, whisking away the lively images, leaving Lydia feeling sullen and often times desperate.

"At last she found herself with child, her hopes rising until she became sick with a fever and lost the baby. Years passed. The chair never rocked, nor did soft lullabies fill the vacant rooms. Instead, Edward and Lydia quarreled over lost dreams and forgotten promises while the relentless wind dragged season after endless season across the God forsaken prairie.

"In time Lydia's heart grew as cold and hard as the unyielding winters and as still and dead as the deep, dark nights that came all too sudden. Life was quickly passing her by. She thought she would go mad. Then fate slipped and dealt her an unexpected turn. She was again with child--her last and only hope."

Iris turned another page where she discovered a lock of fine baby hair. Was it hers? She read on, hoping to find the answer.

"In September of 1852 Lydia gave birth to twin girls, naming them Iris and Ivy. Life seemed worth living after all, that was until Iris developed colic and cried nonstop. No matter how much Lydia consoled or pampered, the baby seemed not to like her. Weeks passed during which Lydia had little or no sleep. Finally she grew despondent and would have nothing to do with Iris. Edward hired a wet-nurse, Lavina Getman, to care for the infant. By the time Iris recovered, Lydia had already concluded that it was only because the baby was glad that her presence was no longer felt in the nursery."

Iris closed her eyes, capturing a sob in her hand. All these years she had blamed herself for her mother's death. Still plagued by guilt, she could hardly bare to read on. Her blurred lashes parted and she gazed at the words that pulled her back to the truth.

"It was a cold November day and a brisk north wind was blowing brittle leaves against the rain spattered window panes. Gazing up at the dismal sky, Lydia's mind conjured up ghostly images of past long, lonely winters. She knew she had to leave, to escape and never come back. He wouldn't miss her if she left Iris for him; Iris who didn't love her anyway.'

"The rest of the story is told in my own words and was not relayed to me by my mistress.

"Lydia waited until nightfall when everyone was asleep, not knowing that, unable to sleep, I watched her from the window in the nursery.

"Having thrown a hooded cloak around her shoulders she crept out of the house and stole across the yard through the windy shadows toward the stable where, it appears, she had instructed a hired man to ready a buggy for her departure. Returning to the house she hastily packed a valise, then hid Ivy inside her cloak and with renewed determination retraced her steps. I saw her climb into the cavity of the waiting buggy. The door thudded shut and the horses lunged forward, clattering off into the darkness. Lydia was gone."

Iris reread the final sentence that had been obscured by her tears. She closed the diary and laid it on the scanty grass in front of the head stone, thinking it was as though she had turned back the pages of time to a place fabricated in someone's morbid imagination. She touched the faded cover, and then opened it, and turning the pages slowly, she knew that what she had read was real, as were the imprints of the dried rose petals and the lock of baby hair that she was now certain was hers. She turned another page and saw a poem about true love. Deciding not to read it she closed the cover. That was her only advantage over the past. She could open or close the book at will. She could turn to the pages that brought her joy, what little joy there was to be had, or indulge in the heart wrenching despair and hopelessness that was her only conception of her mother.

Slumping against the head stone, Iris closed her eyes, remaining oblivious to any movement in the shaded underbrush. The thunder and the waning light had no effect on her as emotions clashed with pre-conceived images in her mind. She had never really thought of her parents discovering one another and falling in love, the way she had fallen so helplessly in love with Andrew. The mere thought of him caused her heart to stumble and she pressed her clenched fist to her tightened lips to suppress a cry. Her heart felt torn in two. As much as it pained her, she was forced to admit that there was nothing her father could have done to make her mother stay.

She stroked the weather worn arch that bore the name of the woman who had rescued her, then died. "I don't even know what you looked like," she wept quietly.

As much as she wanted to remain hidden by the protective shield of the orchard, Iris knew that she must go back home. There was one more thing she needed to do. Wiping her eyes, she got up and taking one last lingering look at the diary she spoke softly, "This doesn't belong to me, or to your mother. It belongs to you."

For a moment she considered the coming rain and the rain and snow that would fall forever until the pages of the diary de-composed and were a part of the earth, the words seeping into the ground where Lavina lay peacefully resting.

"Thank you for telling me the truth," Iris said in a low voice before she turned and walked away.

Retracing her steps, she came upon Honey nuzzling the tall grass near the edge of the road. She untied the reins, then leaning into Honey's warm side she patted her sleek neck. "Oh! I'll be right back," she said softly. She started skirting the edge of the road in search of wildflowers to put on Livvy's grave when she saw a man fast approaching on a horse.

CHAPTER TWENTY-SEVEN

"What are you doing out here? I warned you there might be wild horses running loose." The man on horseback shouted above a low rumbling thunder.

Iris stood up, fastening her gaze on the man riding toward her. Wondering who he was, she pensively turned, craning her neck to see if there was someone on the road behind her. Before she was able to comprehend the situation, the horse came to a staggering halt beside her and a tall, broad-shouldered man silhouetted against a spattering of rumbling clouds quickly bent over and swooped her up off the ground. She was too stunned to scream, a pitiable shriek being the only sound that parted her lips. Before the thought of escape had occurred to Iris, the rider held her in a commanding embrace, angrily spurring the horse into a swift gallop.

As the horse's powerful hooves hammered the road, Iris became enveloped in fear. Fighting to catch her breath, she only succeeded in causing herself to feel light-headed and faint. Panic engulfed her and instinctively she flung her head back, striking the man's massive chest.

Her captor's hold tightened. "What are you doing?" he bellowed, his deep-throated voice full of impatience.

"Put me down!" Iris wailed, the desperate sound of her plea suffocating her further.

When the man failed to comply, Iris weakened and slumped forward, on the verge of crying uncontrollably. A sob escaped her and she clamped her lips tightly together, refusing to give her abductor cause for triumph.

On the edge of ferocity the man replied hotly, "What's gotten into you woman? You're not getting down until I take you home."

Fearing the worst, Iris fought to escape, screaming, "Help! Someone help me!" while struggling to free herself, not caring whether she tumbled to the ground.

Debra L. Hall

With his bristled jaw pushed firmly against her face the man spoke sternly. "Have you gone mad?" His hold tightened until Iris was forced to relent, or faint from lack of air. When she realized that he was headed toward the old Miller place her sense of reason fast gave way to desperation. She began shaking tremulously, a feeling of bitter nausea rising in her throat. The sound of her racing heart echoed in her head, screaming for escape. When they entered the farm yard and Iris saw other horses tied in front of the house, terrifying possibilities instantly took shape in her mind. Gathering what little strength she could muster, she whirled around, swiping at the man's face, heavily shadowed by the wide brim of his Stetson. Cursing, he whipped back the reins and swung from the saddle with Iris' back clamped tight against his broad chest. She jerked forward and bit his forearm. His painful swearing rented the air as he tightened his hold. Iris lashed back, screaming shrilly, kicking until she was certain she had rented a gash in the man's shin. The man snarled angrily. Fumbling to re-position her, he carried her sideways, his arm encircling her waist, his other arm holding her flailing arms at bay. He blundered up the few steps and flung himself against the frail door that flew open, hitting the inside wall with a sound like that of gunfire.

As soon as the man's boots sounded on the wood floor Iris thrashed wildly. Losing his balance the man stumbled, dropping Iris at his feet. There was the sound of running, followed by a dead silence then a long gasp. Iris shakily pushed her loosened hair away from her face and there, gazing back at her with a startled expression was a mirrored image of herself.

Iris drew in a startled breath. "It...it's you," she stammered, on the verge of tears.

"What the hell?" Her captor groaned behind her.

The woman stared unseeingly. "Who are you?" she asked in a voice very near to that of Iris' own.

Iris' aching muscles cinched as she struggled to get up. She fell back against the door frame, fighting to stop the breathless trembling in her voice. "She never told you, did she?"

"Who? What are you talking about?" When Iris failed to reply immediately the woman glared suspiciously at the man, who by now was standing between them.

Seeing the flare in her sister's lavender-blue eyes, Iris thought how alike their expressions were.

Exasperated, Ivy jeered, "Where did you find this woman?"

The man looked dumbfounded at Iris, then back at his wife before offering a defense. "I...I saw her walking on the road and I...I thought she was...you. So I..."

"You abducted her?" Ivy brashly accused, her doubled fists rigidly fixed on her hips.

The man whipped off his hat and slapped it angrily against his thigh. "I said I thought she was you!" He yelled.

"I'm Edward Stratton's daughter...and so are you," Iris responded soberly, her heart swelling.

"Edward Stratton had twins?" The man uttered in disbelief.

Ivy leered sharply at her bewildered husband hovering in front of her. In a careful voice she questioned, "Who's Edward Stratton?"

The man's brow collapsed into a disheartening scowl. Groaning deeply he whirled around and struck the air with his hat. "The only man around who's word alone will have my neck in a noose," he raucously asserted.

Worn down and feeling under great duress, Iris' hand flew to her mouth to stay a cry. Everything in the room suddenly appeared blurred. Another cry rapidly rose from her pained heart and yet still another. Her nerves singed, she was not ready or willing to face another confrontation. Without pause she pushed herself away from the door frame and ran from the room outside into the rain. She heard Ivy call for her to stop before the man's voice rose above the storm:

"Let her go!"

...

Andrew was riding the fence, pulling a line of stray horses, when he saw a horse nibbling grass on the road ahead. Thinking it was strange that a bridled horse would be loose in the rain, he approached slowly, so as not to frighten her. Moving ahead a few steps, he suddenly realized that it was Honey. He looked cautiously about but saw no sign of Iris. Growing concerned, he dismounted and tied his reins and the lead rope to a nearby fence post. With his hand outstretched he walked toward Honey. He squatted down beside her with his knees wide apart; studying the ground for footprints, but the ground was too muddy. Scanning the trees, he rubbed his chin contemplatively. Why would Iris leave Honey untethered in the rain? He stood up, pulled the brim of his Stetson down to keep the rain off of his face then tied the loose reins to a shrub. Taking one last look around, he then decided to search along the road. He swiftly mounted apprehension fast replacing his sense of reasoning.

...

The rain lashed down on Iris' upturned face as she made her way dispiritedly in search of Honey. No longer fighting the urge to cry, she wept openly as she plodded down the muddy road. A short time passed when, through the dispersed light ahead, she saw a farm wagon approaching slowly. She was barely able to make out the shape of, what appeared to be a man sitting hunched over on the seat with a blanket draped around his shoulders to protect himself from the rain. As the wagon drew nearer she saw that a canvas had been spread over the bed of the wagon and, deciding that he must be a tinker, she waved for him to stop.

Veering the reins to one side, the driver brought the wagon to a slow halt under an over hanging bough near the edge of the road. With her head bent away from the wind, Iris stepped around the many rain-filled ruts until she was close enough for the man to hear her when she spoke.

"Hello. Sir, can you help me?"

"Well, look at what I found here," the man chortled softly

to himself.

When he raised his head, his fierce eyes level with the rim of his slouch hat, Iris immediately recognized Leo Branson's despicable grin. She instantly felt her head careening as a deep chill flew down her spine. Without pause, she turned and sprang like a wildcat toward the darkness of the trees. She scrambled down the sodden embankment, adrenalin shooting through her like a prairie fire. She broke into a stumbling run, anxious to reach the density of the trees. Leo was quick on her heels, snatching her by the arm and flinging her around ready and willing to grapple with her.

Exhausted from the day's events, there was no room in Iris' mind for alarm. For a dreadful moment she feared there was no getting away. Suddenly an intense hatred for what he had done to her father ignited a raging fire inside of her. Though she felt imprisoned by his grip, she lashed out, her fists doubled. Leo caught the wide blow she flung at his head. He struck her back, leaving her stunned. He grabbed a fist full of her hair and snapped her head back. Gasping, she felt herself near hysteria. She forced down the screams that surged to her throat, and yet was unable to hold back a feeble cry. With his face close to hers, Leo's gaze narrowed above her eyes, his wiry brows growing stiff.

"Ya' ain't so naive that ya' thought I was just takin' a little drive in the rain are ya'? To tell ya' the truth Missy, which I know's important to your kind, I was goin' courtin', and you're just the little lady I was holdin' out for."

"I'll see you dead first," Iris scoffed. Spitting angrily in his face, she flung at him with her fist clenched while she jabbed at him with her feet. Leo fumbled madly in an effort to cinch her wrists when Iris swung hard at his face with her open palm, striking his eye. Leo's face flared an angry mottled red, the cynical glint in his eyes sending a horrifying tremor through Iris' body.

In one swift move, Leo had Iris pinned to the ground. "Let me give it to ya' straight, Missy." He reached inside his pocket and brought out a pen knife. Flipping out the blade he held it in front of Iris' face. His eyes examined the rain speckled edge. "I got plans for ya'," he stated matter-of-factly. "I'm takin' ya' to town where we're gonna git married proper like, so's no one can accuse me of not bein' a gentleman." His mouth turned down. "It's too bad we're not in your aunt's cozy parlor where we can sit and discuss our weddin', the way it was takin' shape in the first place." He looked up at the rumbling clouds and jeered. "This is your own doin', ya'know that don't ya'? I was willin' to court ya' like a real gentleman but ya' had to have it your way. Now ya' forced me to take matters into my own hands."

Holding her down with his wide hand, Leo clamped the knife between his crooked teeth then wrested himself from the ground. When he yanked Iris to her feet she screamed in pain and he flew around, swearing viciously. She fell back, unnerved by the nearness of him. "Shut up!" he growled savagely, his lurid eyes penetrating her. "There ain't no one out here to hear your pitiful pleas for help."

Iris braced herself defiantly, her feet fixed firmly to the ground. "I won't marry you! You can't make me," she vehemently hissed.

Leo whirled around and struck her, knocking her to the ground where he fell with a thump beside her, his breath hot on her burning cheek, the knife now pressed tautly to her chin. "Your tongue's not as sharp as this blade. Want to see?" In one swift move he slashed off a good six inches of her hair. She cried out, her eyes closed tightly, her chest heaving sporadically.

Leo eyed her narrowly. "That's just for starters." He paused to look up at the murky sky. "I think we have an understanding now, don't we, Missy?"

Cringing beneath his morbid touch, Iris struggled with every breath she took. Unable to speak, she nodded rapidly.

"Good." Leo closed the knife and shoved it back into his pocket. "Now, come on," he ordered gruffly. Lifting Iris off the ground he flung her over his shoulder.

They were in the wagon, her pinned beside him by his

claw-like grip on her knee, when Iris realized that he fully intended on going through with his sinister wedding plan. She had to get away. But how? It was raining heavily, and no one would be out on the road, especially once it got dark. Leo picked up the reins. She knew she had to act swiftly or never see her family again. She glanced anxiously over her shoulder where she saw a rock holding down a corner of the crumpled canvas. Without stopping to reconsider, she wrenched sharply from his hold, grabbed the rock and, jumping up, she flung herself at him, striking him on the side of the head. He let out a derisive snort and flew back, shoving her violently with his outstretched arm. She screamed as she flew over the side of the wagon. Tumbling down the embankment she struck her head, losing consciousness.

CHAPTER TWENTY-EIGHT

Andrew heard a scream and, sure that it was Iris, he spurred his horse into a gallop. Just down the road he saw a man draped in a blanket standing upright in a farm wagon. He knew at once, by the immense form that it was Leo Branson. In the same instant Leo caught sight of Andrew and he feverishly pulled a rifle from under the canvas. Rapidly cocking it, he fired. The bullet whizzed by Andrew's head, searing a path along his jaw. Andrew grunted against the intense pain while he whipped his rifle from the scabbard, cocked the lever action, took a quick aim, and fired back. At the sound of the explosive cross fire, Leo's horse reared, then lunged, jerking the wagon and hurling Leo backwards onto the road where he landed with a deadening thump.

His rifle cocked, Andrew goaded his horse into a gentle gait until he was near enough to spot Leo's trigger finger. There was no movement, which meant nothing to Andrew. He'd seen men left for dead after a dual, then when the shooter's back was turned the gunfire started in earnest.

He approached the wagon with some trepidation, murmuring softly to Leo's horse. Afraid that he would find Iris dead, he fearfully eyed the bed of the wagon. His heart hammering inside his chest, he lifted the crinkled edge of the canvas. Seeing a worn pair of boots and a battered box of shells he let out a short gasp and threw back the covering. Relieved, a chill raced down his spine while his breath escaped him in a rush. He swallowed hard, fighting for air. There was nothing but a bed roll and a few boxes of canned goods. Visibly shaken, Andrew quickly looked around. Iris couldn't be far. The wagon had only moved a few feet since he heard her scream. Disgruntled, he frowned. He wondered if Leo had been heading for home, which led him to conclude that Leo's father might be hiding somewhere in the trees with a rifle aimed at his head. Neither one of the Branson's was so ignorant they wouldn't know that the law would be hunting them after Leo's last attack on Iris.

Andrew dismounted in a wide swoop, his rifle pointed at Leo's expansive back. When he was near enough he reached out and pinned Leo to the ground with his rifle. He was sure Leo was dead. With the tip of his rain spattered boot he rolled the body over. Leo's head lolled to one side and a runnel of water, that had gathered in Andrew's hat brim, spattered on his grotesque face.

"You went and broke your neck didn't you?" Andrew jeered, pushing the lifeless form with the heel of his boot before he turned and walked away.

Rid of the assailant, Andrew skimmed through the underbrush along the road searching for Iris. Being alert for any signs of movement in the woods beyond, he started when he saw what he thought was a shallow pool of water at the foot of the slope. The idea of blue water refused to register in his mind. He knew instantly that what he was seeing was the reflection of Iris' blue shirt, the same one she had worn the first time he saw her disguised as a man charging down Stoney Creek Road.

Fear stricken, he scudded down the embankment, stammering incoherent words of gratitude when he saw that she wasn't laying face down in the water. He dropped to his knees beside her, his eyes burning with tears at the sight of her eye that was swollen shut, along with the deep bruises on her face, and her severed hair that was plastered with mud and leaves. Laying his ear over her heart he heard a faint pattering. "Thank God!" he whispered, his lips briefly touching hers.

She whimpered when he swept her drenched body into his arms. He pressed her gently against his chest, gripping the back of her shirt, afraid that if he let go she would leave him forever.

"I'm sorry," he faltered. "I'm so sorry. I'll never leave you alone again. Please forgive me, Iris."

Logic forced back his emotion, replacing the fear in his heart with much needed courage. Mounting the embankment, with Iris nestled helplessly in his arms; he thought how glad he was that Leo Branson was dead. It would prevent him from going to jail for murdering the bastard.

...

Iris slipped in and out of consciousness throughout the stormy night, her restless dreams mingling with reality. She was vaguely aware of her aunt's presence, her low voice fraught with worry as she bathed Iris. Stella appeared in the room, uttering remorseful words of regret. Her strong hands cradled Iris' head gently while her aunt's slender fingers washed the debris from her hair. Her aunt was talking about lavender and Iris began dreaming of spring and curtains fluffing above the herb garden. Katie's light footsteps scurried across the floor then pattered back. The sharp, dry scent of lavender steeped in tepid water filled Iris' head just before she felt the lavender rain slipping through her hair, calming her, making her sleep.

There was the sound of someone tapping lightly on the door. She recognized Hickory's voice. Her own voice sounded dry and brittle. "I want...that," she whimpered, "on the book." He handed her what he thought was the trinket she had asked for. Iris tried to open her eyes but there was no movement, nothing.

"I found the doctor," Hickory said in a low voice that was full of anxious concern.

Someone was touching her. A man. It wasn't Andrew. She knew his touch. Large, gentle hands examined her body that throbbed with pain. The dark shape eased several drops of tart, burning draught between her slightly parted swollen lips then turned his back that was like a wall to her, and began to speak to a huddled man whose face showed distorted signs of distress. "Broken ribs...fractured collar bone, dislocated arm.. badly sprained ankle." The man disappeared. Someone was crying. It was her father.

A day drifted by. Iris could tell by the light that appeared, waned, and then subtly slipped away. It wasn't raining anymore. The air was full of the sound of locust. Oblivious to all that took place downstairs, she heard muddled bits and pieces of the goings on in the Stratton household. Across the dimly lit room, she saw Brenton Hadley holding her aunt. Were his hands touching her face? Did he really kiss her? Was it him that said, 'Don't worry Sweetheart?' or was it a dream playing out in Iris' drugged mind? It was too real. She felt herself wanting to smile.

The shadows in the room darkened. Someone lit the lamp. A pensive man, her father, stood over her bed. Iris saw herself standing beside him. But it wasn't her at all. She lay numb at the bottom of the embankment, crying. The man embraced the woman who was the image of herself, her sister, and a feeling of warmth spread throughout Iris' body, healing her. She struggled to see more clearly the man with bittersweet tears in his eyes when, suddenly, another man appeared behind him. Her father called him John. He was the man she fought with, the man who led her to discover her sister: Ivy on the wall, the baby who was snatched from her side sixteen years ago.

Afraid, Iris fell into a whirling darkness. She dreamt of the cradle in the attic, its cavernous depth full of distorted faces writhing from Livvy's diary.

...

Andrew sat helpless on the edge of a straight-back chair beside Iris' bed, his elbows fixed on his spread knees, his forehead resting on the heels of his hands. His teeth clenched at the thought of Leo Branson's despicable hands causing the dark blotches on Iris' ivory face. Reaching out, he took her folded hand in his. Her fingers slid open and he saw a button pressed tightly into her palm. His jaw cinched hard, staying his tears, just before his lips lightly touched hers. Tormented by her lack of expression, he willed her to come back to him, promising to erase all her fears, never regretting for a moment that Leo was lying on the side of the road with no one to attend to him but the wolves.

...

It was deep into the following morning, a few hours before dawn, when Iris opened her eyes and was greeted by the moon. Its soothing light had crept through the curtain where it sought the opposite wall and was engaged with a slight breeze in a fanciful game of charades. While searching for familiar images, she was calmed by the delicate enactment. She watched for some time, imagining herself a bride shrouded in the Brussels lace pattern. She heard the sound of footsteps and turned her head slowly, mindful of the intense pain.

"Andrew," she said in a dry, coarse whisper, unused to speaking.

Her aunt immediately appeared at her side, a web shawl wrapped tightly around her shoulders. She picked up Iris' hand. Even though groggy-eyed, Iris saw how serene and full of relief her aunt's face looked.

"He'll be back, dear," her aunt spoke in a careful, guarded voice. "He's gone to check on the herd." She lightly stroked Iris' forehead with her fingertips. "He's been here every minute. He even slept on the floor." An unexpected giggle escaped her. "Miss Bishop would be green with envy if she knew." She struggled to compose herself, then pressing her fingertips to her trembling lips she managed to say, "You look like you're feeling somewhat better."

Iris struggled to smile, every move sending pain through her.

"I have some good news for you," Aunt Emma smiled back. "Andrew's made it known to your father that he means to marry you as soon as he returns, hoping of course that you would be awake by then." Her eyes glinting with tears she audibly whispered. "He'll be happy to see that his wish has come true."

Iris blinked back her tears of joy. "I want to...say yes to him, Aunt Emma."

Emma regarded her niece with renewed pride. "I'm sorry that I ever tried to dissuade you. Andrew's a good man. He needs to know that you'll be safe."

"Leo..."

Emma quickly shook her head. "Leo's dead. He tried to kill Andrew. He fell off his wagon and broke his neck."

Iris released a prolonged sigh.

There was a moment of meditative silence before Emma

lowered her head. "I'm sorry that I never told you about...about Ivy." She pressed her lips tightly together and their eyes met again. "I love you with all my heart and I... would never do...do anything to hurt you. I...I thought I was doing the right thing. I meant to..."

Before she could go on Iris squeezed her hand, her head shaking slowly from side to side. "I don't blame you, Aunt Emma. It's...not your fault. I...I was selfish to...be angry at you when you gave up your whole...life for me."

Emma drew her clustered fingertips under her weighted lashes and a stream of tears trickled onto their joined hands. "I did it because I wanted to, and I'd do it again. I would, Iris, I want you to know that."

Iris gathered a shaky breath. "That's why I love you, and why I'll always need you in my life."

There was a moment of tender silence when Iris glanced at the wall where the moonlight had been replaced by a slight amber hue. The faint light of early dawn began to slip through the lace design searching for its place on the wall opposite her bed. Iris smiled, happy that so many things never changed.

"I saw my sister. I saw Ivy," her words rushed, full of emotion.

Emma nodded rapidly, tightening her shawl. She smiled, seemingly pleased. "I know, dear. She told us."

"She's here?"

"Not now, it's late." Emma laughed. "I guess it's early by now. But she'll be back."

"Has she been here a long time, I mean in Nebraska?" Iris asked.

Emma shook her head slightly. "No. John Stevens met her in Boston, where they were married. When he came back, she came ahead of the herd."

Realizing that Iris was growing tired, Emma patted her hand, ready to leave when Iris cupped her aunt's fingers and Emma looked back at her.

"Is...Rebecca home?"

Aunt Emma smiled thinly while reaching inside her pocket. "She sent you a letter. Would you like for me to read it to you?"

Iris nodded weakly.

It was a short letter. "Dear Iris, I'm sorry I didn't say good-bye. I hope you'll forgive me, but with the drive and all, there just wasn't time. Todd and I were married in Council Bluffs last Friday. We'll be home in a week or so.

"I hope that you don't think badly of Todd. He intends to pay Mr. Stevens back the money he gave to him to go on the drive. Please be happy for me. Your friend, Rebecca."

Iris was happy for Rebecca. She was only sorry that her happiness would be marred when she returned home to discover that her mother had lost a baby. "Do...do her parents...know?" Iris asked her aunt.

Emma nodded.

"Is...Beth okay?"

"It'll take some time, but she'll do all right. Which reminds me. If you'll be getting married this afternoon I'd better get busy. Besides, you need to rest. First your father wants to see you. He told me to wake him as soon as you opened your eyes." Emma bent over and kissed Iris' forehead. "He's better, Iris. The shock of almost losing you brought him back to us. He's talking much better." She smiled faintly. "I was so worried about you."

Iris nodded caringly and her aunt quickly patted her hand before bustling out of the room.

...

Iris could hear her father coming down the hall. She was anxious to see him, to tell him not to worry, that she was going to be okay. She wanted to tell him that she was getting married.

When her father stopped beside the bed, Iris could tell at once by the sorrowful look in his eyes that he was ridden with guilt. She reached up to him and he took her hand.

"I'm going to...be okay, Father." She smiled reassuringly. "Aunt Emma...said so, and we always have to...do whatever she tells us to...do, right."

Blinking back his tears, her father bowed his head. "When Andrew brought you...home and...and I saw what that scum did to you I...I thought I was going to...to lose you." He caught a sob in his throat and swallowed hard.

Iris' heart sank, knowing how difficult it was for her father to tell her the truth after all these years.

"I wanted so badly to tell you...that I was sorry. I never meant to...hurt you or to..."

Iris shook her head. "You didn't hurt me...Father. There was...nothing you could have done to...make her stay. I know that now."

Her father fingered the edge of the embroidered pillow slip Iris was lying on. "I wanted to make...her stay," he said in a sad voice. "I tried Iris; with all my might I...I tried. But she left anyway. All these years I just kept on...pretending that she was still here, in this...house, in the rose garden, in my...heart. I never let...let Emma change a thing, just hoping Lydia would come back to re...claim what we...once had together." He looked back at Iris. "The other day, just after you...left, Mr. Hadley came by with word that...she's on her way, she coming back."

There was an apprehensive pause when neither one knew what to say. Her father searched her face. Iris knew that he was hoping for some sign of acceptance. Not knowing why her mother was coming back, she wasn't sure how to respond.

"I hope you'll...understand," he said with a measure of certainty. "That I have to...try to win her back."

"I know that she once loved you...very much." Iris said, her voice growing tired. "I...I won't hold...it against you, Father."

"Thank you," her father spoke softly next to her ear just before he kissed her forehead. "You need to rest." He smiled down at her. "I understand there's going to be...a wedding this afternoon."

A peaceful blanket spread itself over her and Iris smiled and closed her eyes. The last thing she remembered was hearing the sound of her father's footsteps just before the door clicked shut.

...

In her sleep, Iris heard Andrew whispering next to her ear.

"I love you, Iris, and I want you to marry me this afternoon. I need you to be my wife. I love..." She lifted her lashes and saw Andrew's tender eyes looking down at her. "...you too much to live without you." He smiled wantingly.

"I do," Iris said, half asleep.

"You're getting ahead of yourself, Honey."

Realizing what she'd said Iris giggled with her eyes closed.

"Are you that eager to marry me?"

Iris nodded drowsily, reaching out until their hands met and she brought Andrew's hand to her lips.

"I'm glad because I already told the minister to be here at four o'clock."

"How did...you know I'd say yes?"

"I had a suspicion that you couldn't live without me either. We need each other, Iris. I knew it the first day I saw you."

...

It was a simple wedding. Iris wasn't dressed like a Bostonian bride, the kind her aunt used to tell her about when she was growing up. Instead, her aunt produced a bed jacket trimmed in Alencon lace for her to wear over her simple night gown, and a Chantilly lace veil was draped lightly over her head. With Andrew beside her she felt as beautiful and tender as the prairie in spring.

Andrew sat beside her at the head of the bed, dressed in dark twill trousers, a midnight blue shirt that Ida had pressed for him, with a black string tie and polished boots. His brushed hat was propped on the bed post behind him.

No one seemed to care that her face was bruised or that his jaw showed signs of gun battle. Aunt Emma stood longingly beside Iris' proud father who was seated and Brenton Hadley stood notably at Emma's opposite side near a stand of cascading ferns, while holding her hand in the folds of her garnet colored skirt. Ivy stood next to her husband, John Stevens who stood beside his father, Jacob. Just outside the small cluster, Stella, Ida, Hickory and Katie huddled near the doorway.

After a brief ceremony, vows were exchanged, the cherished words whispered between them. Andrew slipped his grandmother's wedding band from his little finger and slid it onto his bride's finger, their lips brushing lightly as he did so. They were pronounced man and wife and the room filled with joyous clapping followed by the murmur of happy voices.

While the family and added guests attended a wedding supper downstairs, Andrew and Iris were left alone, Stella having prepared a beautiful supper tray that was sent to their room.

No sooner had the guests departed when there was a slight knock on the door. The door opened a crack, a package was quickly slipped into the room and the door closed. Andrew brought the package to the bed where he helped Iris open it. Her lips pressed into a trembling smile when she saw the completed sketch of the windmill.

"He finished it," she wept.

Andrew brushed her tears. "He said he would, didn't he?"

It was nearing dusk and the room was growing dim. Andrew could see that Iris was over tired. They were too happy and too in love to be hungry so they laid back into the pillows. "You need to rest," he said, removing her veil.

Andrew covered his face with his hat, his arms folded over his chest; he crossed his boots at the foot of the bed, while Iris moved as close to his side as she could.

"I'll always love you, Iris," he whispered huskily.

"And I'll always love you," Iris answered him sleepily, "like the prairie, far reaching and as tender as a wildflower in spring."

Turning toward one another, their lips met before their

faces touched and they fell asleep. A soft breeze parted the curtains where the fireflies lingered and came to rest on Andrew's hand that lay protectively over Iris' heart.

About the Author

Debra L. Hall lives in Nebraska with her husband of twenty-four years. They have two sons. Debra, a member of the Nebraska Writer's Guild, has receiver awards for published poetry and is the author of two Historicals, The Easterner, (available through 1stBooks Library) and Texas Wildflower. She has a published non-fiction article on A.H.D.H. (Attention Deficit Hyperactivity Disorder), both the latter available by e-mailing sylviasloan@cox.net. Debra has also lectured students on critiquing fiction and poetry. She is presently working on several chapter books for children. Watch for Debra's next book, A.D.D. and ME, A rhyme for families, teachers, and children, written from a child's viewpoint and formatted in scrapbook form.

LaVergne, TN USA
10 November 2010
204206LV00001B/7/A